ENDGAME

STAR TREK VOYAGER®
ENDGAME

A Novelization by Diane Carey
Based on ENDGAME
Teleplay by Kenneth Biller & Robert Doherty
Story by Rick Berman &
Kenneth Biller & Brannon Braga

and
HOMECOMING
by Christie Golden

Based upon STAR TREK®
created by Gene Roddenberry,
and STAR TREK: VOYAGER
created by Rick Berman & Michael Piller
& Jeri Taylor

POCKET BOOKS
NEW YORK   LONDON   TORONTO   SYDNEY   SINGAPORE

An *Original* Publication of POCKET BOOKS

POCKET BOOKS, a division of Simon & Schuster, Inc.
1230 Avenue of the Americas, New York, NY 10020

ISBN: 0-7434-4216-4

First Pocket Books trade paperback printing July 2001

10   9   8   7   6   5   4

POCKET and colophon are registered trademarks of Simon & Schuster, Inc.

Printed in the U.S.A.

To Jeff "Vern" Archer:
For all the help and enthusiasm: Thanks!

ENDGAME

CHAPTER 1

FIREWORKS BROKE HIGH ACROSS THE INVERTED REFLECTION OF THE city lights on black water. San Francisco Bay shimmered with colored streams and rediscovered the night sky. On the newly refurbished Golden Gate Bridge, an icon so long established that no one could imagine these waters without the great suspended structure, thousands upon thousands of spectators cheered at the spectacular explosions in the sky. The city in its dazzling livery, millions of jewel-like lights bundled into geometric shapes, began to flicker on and off from building to building in a coordinated tribute. Though the bridge was old and the fireworks an ancient art, this was a supremely modern scene that could only happen in a population center.

Out of the gauzy clouds the enormous cetacean body of the starship swept downward, almost touching the teaming balustrades, only to rise at the last moment. The reflection of her nacelles glowed brightly in the gunmetal water below as her oblong primary hull rose to blow the geodesic fireworks into a blizzard.

On the bridge, the crowd roared and waved their arms wildly.

The ship passed over their heads in a tidy maneuver, came about, and made another pass.

The starship looked somewhat old-fashioned now despite the patches of alien armor defiantly fixed to a quarter of her hull area, and the other three-quarters scratched and scarred by turmoil. She was like an old warhorse, still holding her head up despite her bleeding flanks and ratted mane.

"These should be familiar images to everyone who remembers the *U.S.S. Voyager*'s triumphant return to Earth after twenty-three years in the Delta Quadrant. *Voyager* captivated the hearts and minds of people throughout the Federation, so it seems fitting that on the tenth anniversary of their return we take a moment to recall the sacrifices made by the crew."

The newscaster wasn't very inspiring. Maybe he'd overrehearsed.

Still, quite a show. That business of the city lights' flashing in a coordinated performance was a new thing. Well, new ten years ago.

Ten years. Seemed like forty.

And twenty-six years in space, lost, toying daily with hopelessness, struggle, challenge, isolation . . . *whush.*

Funny how the toughest tests in life could turn out to be the best part of life. The things people often said they wanted most—peace and quiet, easy advancement, security—weren't really the most satisfying experiences after all, or the ones that kept people together.

Thus, nostalgia. Kathryn Janeway found herself peeling back the pages of her life to that stressful quarter century rushing at high warp through the Delta Quadrant, out of place, away from comfort, without help, struggling by the day to keep a ship and crew together with a single ideal and making sure that ideal didn't fade.

4

Had she been right or wrong to push them onward? There had been other civilizations they could've joined, lived out a life on some nice planet, more fulfilled, have other careers, more family, a chance to be captains themselves if they wanted. Maybe if she'd known then about the twenty-three years . . .

Oh, how old was that question? Older than the whole voyage, now. Old and shriveled. She'd combed her hair with it every morning since the ship found itself propelled seventy thousand light-years into deep space with no shortcut home. She'd made a decision and stuck with it. Why look back now?

But twenty-six years . . .

She picked up her old coffee cup, one of the last links to her great long struggle, and turned it a little to avoid the chip in the rim. Six times she'd had to rescue this cup from attentive yeomen who wanted to get her a new one.

"Earlier today in the Tri-Nebulas," the newscaster went on, "corruption charges were brought against a Ferengi gaming consortium—"

"Computer, end display."

Janeway stood up from her Victorian couch and moved past the Bombay wicker table to the vast curved window. In the soft glass she caught a faint echo of her silver-streaked hair and rather liked the image. Maybe she was indulging herself with a touch of vanity, but other than the streaks, she thought she hadn't changed that much. A few lines here and there—a few.

Beyond the reflection lay the always stunning expanse of San Francisco Bay and the bridge. This fan-shaped wing of apartment buildings had been architecturally designed to give all residents this view. It had become a favorite living space for many admirals who wanted to remain close to Starfleet Command but not live on the grounds. To Janeway, though, the bridge and the bay meant something more, she truly believed, than to all the other admirals. At least something different.

She hoped that after today it would still mean something good.

Invasion.

Another reunion.

The apartment was filled now with people, all kinds of people, human and alien, young and old, Starfleet and otherwise—the surviving members of the _Voyager_'s crew and their families. Thank God some of them had enough time left to have families. Drinks and hors d'oeuvres, soft music, laughter, some smiles. Janeway hovered behind the umbrella tree and watched as one of the kids approached Harry Kim and tapped his arm, breaking a conversation he was having with somebody else.

Kim was a Starfleet captain now with his own starship, the only one of the remaining crew who had pursued such command. The studious effort had taken him a while and grayed his hair, but he'd made it. Oh, yes, Janeway had to admit to herself that she'd pushed a few buttons for him, and he had a leg-up just from the _Voyager_'s reputation. Why not?

"Hello," Kim said to the child at his elbow.

"What's your name?" the little girl asked.

"Harry. What's yours?"

"Sabrina."

"Naomi's daughter? You've gotten so big?"

"I don't remember you."

"I haven't been to one of these reunions in four years." Kim straightened, rather proudly. "I've been on a deep-space assignment."

"For four years?"

Janeway smiled. To a child, this was eternity.

"Compared to how long I was on *Voyager,* it seemed like a long weekend. Can you find your mother for me? I'd love to say hello."

The little girl nodded and merrily departed, giving Janeway her opening. She wanted to talk to Kim, but only to him, not to a knot of smiling relatives trying to pretend they were having a great time—again.

"Here you are, Captain," she began, circling in on Kim with a fresh drink for him.

"Thank you, Admiral." Kim nodded toward the little girl. "I haven't seen her since she was a baby."

"It's amazing how fast you've all grown up," Janeway said.

Kim shrugged, then his smile faded. "How's Tuvok?"

"The same." She wanted to tell him the truth, but this was more gentle.

His expression suggested he knew more than he was saying. "I thought maybe I'd go see him tomorrow."

"That would be nice."

And it would be nice if we were more honest with each other.

"I'm sorry I missed the funeral," Kim went on. "I should've been there."

Janeway took his hand. "You were on a mission. Everyone understood." They looked at each other in mutual discomfort, but with genuine affection too. "It's good to see you, Harry."

She started to say more, but her throat closed up. There was no clever way, after all. How could she tell him she needed him and his ship out of her way?

This reunion was the tenth time she'd fielded these awful sensations, so much that she had come to dread such events. People had been kind and generous, certainly . . . she'd been given citation after medal after doctorate after award, and each one diminished her sense of accomplishment. As she glanced around at the

7

faces of her crew, her friends, the awareness of being a cele-
brated central figure in this great drama of space exploration
pressed her again with the feeling that she'd failed. She couldn't
shake it.

Every time they had a reunion, they wanted to feel more like
they were home, and every time satisfaction slipped a little farther away. They'd been lost for twenty-six years, the prime of
each of their lives. When they'd returned, their families had
grown, died, changed, forgotten, or dreamed of possibilities no
longer possible. The *Voyager* had done the impossible—it had
come back from the dead.

The crew had stayed dead.

She had brought them back, but too late. Though she had
dreaded this reunion, it galvanized her sense of purpose. Her
mission wasn't over.

CHAPTER 2

THIS PARTICULAR REUNION WAS MORE TROUBLING THAN THE OTH-
ers. Janeway moved away from Harry Kim without saying what
she had planned to say. She'd given him plenty of orders in the
past and demanded he not question her judgment or plans, but
today he was a Starfleet captain and things were more complicated. He had a right to ask why. She wasn't ready to tell.

She floated about the room, attending everyone but not really
engaging in conversation. She was going through the motions.
They all were.

Pretending to involve herself with a small crystal plate of
munchies, she paused and watched as Tom Paris went to answer
the apartment door. In his New York casuals and with those sil-
ver temples, he had a Dashiell Hammett look about him these
days—she suspected he worked on it. Well, why not?

"Doc!" Paris exclaimed in an "about time" tone.

Through the door came *Voyager*'s one-of-a-kind shipboard
physician, looking exactly as he did the first day he was activated. Holograms had that advantage—eternal life. Dressed in

civilian duds, the Doctor entered with a young woman on his arm, definitely a source of curiosity for Janeway and everyone. After all . . .

"Mr. Paris," the Doctor greeted merrily, and drew Paris into a particularly casual hug. "Where have you been hiding yourself?"

"I've been busy."

"A new holonovel?"

Paris smiled, not without pride. "I'll be sure to get your input before I send it to my publisher. Aren't you going to introduce me to your date?"

"Tom Paris," the Doctor said, beaming, "say hello to Lana, my blushing bride."

Paris couldn't control this particular expression. "You're married?"

"Tomorrow's our two-week anniversary," Lana said. A musical voice, for sure.

"Congratulations!" Paris absorbed the news, then huffed, "I guess my invitation got lost in subspace?"

"You should be flattered," the Doctor said. "We took a page out of your book and eloped."

Lana eyed her husband. "Joe has a real flare for romantic gestures."

"Joe?"

"I decided I couldn't get married without a name," the Doctor clarified.

Paris struck an expression. "It took you thirty-three years to come up with 'Joe'?"

"It was Lana's grandfather's name."

"Oh . . . so you're not . . ." Paris looked at the girl, and from behind the couch Janeway buried a chuckle. She'd had the same question and probably the same look on her face when she first heard about this. *What kind of a woman marries a computer-generated—*

"A hologram?" Lana finished for him. "No."

The Doctor raised his chin. "Frankly, Mr. Paris, I'm surprised you'd even ask. I thought we were beyond those sorts of distinctions."

"Are you kidding?" Paris lit up. "I think it's great! I'm in a 'mixed marriage' myself, remember?"

"Speaking of which, where is that wife of yours?"

Janeway took that as a cue and turned into the outer corridor of the spacious apartment. "They're looking for you," she said.

In the corridor, B'Elanna Torres peeked out and gestured her closer.

"Why are you hiding back here?" Janeway asked.

B'Elanna eyed the doorway. "The Doctor's new 'wife.' How can he have a wife? I can't get used to it."

"As far as we can detect, he qualifies as a life-form. You know that."

"Oh, I *know* it . . . I just can't *feel* it yet. Do I have to get used to everything? *Everything?"*

"No, I suppose not. When did you get back?"

"Just this morning. I had to arrange for two special transports and one stowaway leg just to get here tonight."

"Good thing," Janeway said. "If you'd missed the reunion, Harry would've started asking questions."

"Not to mention my loving husband, the curious Captain Proton. It always makes him nervous when I have to tap my Klingon blood."

"Don't tap his curiosity, whatever you do," Janeway warned.

B'Elanna eyed her. "You'll have to be careful too. There are rumors starting to flitter about those conversions you're making to your personal shuttle. You might have to make up a new story."

"Never mind the shuttle for now. It's almost finished anyway, and I'll have it moved before inspections. What did you accomplish? Am I in?"

"The High Council had a lot of questions."

"What did you tell them?"

"The truth," B'Elanna said with a shrug, "with a Klingon twist. I told them my beloved former captain, who saved my life many times in glorious battle, would consider it an honor to submit Korath's House for consideration."

Janeway pushed down a twinge of worry. This couldn't be so easy. "Do you think it'll work?"

"I'm just the Federation liaison," B'Elanna downplayed, "but I'd like to think I have some influence. You still haven't told me why you're trying to help Korath."

"He's an old friend."

Fibs, lies, deceptions, and redirections. How much could she protect her friends—the real ones—from what she planned to do?

B'Elanna didn't buy it. "Would this 'old friend' have anything to do with the mission you sent my daughter on?"

Janeway hid her misgivings in a smile. "Sorry, B'Elanna, but you know I can't talk about that."

Can't, won't—small distinction.

"Couldn't you at least have delayed it till after the reunion? She really wanted to be here."

"She'll be home soon," Janeway said, answering the question B'Elanna was actually asking. "I promise."

"May I have everyone's attention, please? Attention!"

A spoon clinked madly upon a champagne glass on the other side of the living room. Janeway and Torres turned and stepped out of their hiding place in the hallway, to see Reg Barclay quieting the gathering so he could make his announcement. In his uniform, with the rank of commander, he seemed at ease in front of a crowd—quite saying something for Reginald Barclay.

"Ten years ago tonight," Barclay began with a touch of drama, "this crew returned home from the longest away mission in Starfleet history. Twenty-three years together made you a family . . . one I'm proud to have been adopted by. So let's raise our glasses—to the journey."

"To the journey!"

Around the room glasses clinked and smiles flickered.

Admiral Janeway raised her own glass too, but she didn't drink to that toast. She had one of her own.

"And," she began firmly, "to those of us who aren't here to celebrate it with us."

As around her the extended family of *Voyager* affirmed her sentiment, Janeway pressed her lips to the glass and blocked the rest of her statement with a sip of champagne. Better buried in bubbles than spoken yet . . .

May things change for them and for all of us, suddenly and soon.

CHAPTER 3

"LADIES AND GENTLEMEN . . . MEET THE BORG."

The Borg. Still, after decades, a terrorizing presence that had yet to be subdued. Some neighbors you could live with. Others—

A Borg drone shimmered into formation at Commander Barclay's summons. Bulky and robotic, the drone had just enough left of the humanoid element to be essentially paralyzing at first, second, and third glance. They were a ghastly-looking bunch, the Borg, with their underlying living body infected with mechanics, threaded with artifice down to the last fiber, until they didn't even need blood anymore.

Yet, there were those eyes . . . impenetrable, uninfluenced.

The old Pathfinder research lab, once used for radical communications to call out to the lost *Voyager,* had been converted into a classroom. The Borg hologram rotated gracelessly before a cluster of Starfleet Academy cadets on tiered seats. Some of the kids flinched at the sight—and it was indeed harrowing.

And even more for someone who had dealt with the Borg, as

Kathryn Janeway had. She sat on the dais while Barclay continued addressing his class.

"Over the course of this term, you're going to become intimately familiar with the Collective. You'll learn about the assimilation process, the Borg hierarchy, the psychology of the hive
mind."

Barclay paused, letting those words sink in, for they had great
eternal significance even though they were spoken quickly.
Assimilation . . . the hive . . . what a civilization!

Janeway repressed a shiver.

"When it comes to your performance in this class," Barclay
went on, enjoying himself, "my expectations are no different
than those of the Borg Queen herself . . . perfection."

Several cadets laughed, breaking the sensation of impending
doom always brought on by the sight of a Borg, and the mere
idea of their queen.

"This semester," Barclay continued, "we're very fortunate to
have a special guest lecturer, the woman who literally 'wrote the
book' on the Borg. Admiral Kathryn Janeway."

Janeway smiled, but not because of the applause. Poor
Barclay, always pontificating for effect—Janeway hadn't really
written a book. Didn't he know what "literally" meant? Oh,
well, if he weren't trying too hard, he wouldn't be Reg Barclay.

Speaking before groups of all kinds from students to Rotary
Clubs, support leagues to historical societies, had lost its gloss
for her years before. The sheer redundancy of the questions quite
effectively offset the hero worship. Certainly she appreciated
being treated so well, and understood the need of others to focus
their own dreams, their fears, and needs for a happy ending.

Ten years made for a lot of public appearances.

She stood up to the applause of the starstruck children of

Starfleet's near future. Before very long, these would be the helmsmen and spectrographers and analysts and officers of the next batch of Starfleet ships spreading out into the settled galaxy to discover the new and tend the established.

Most of them didn't even shave yet.

"Thank you," she said when the applause settled. "I'm glad to be here . . . a question already, Cadet?"

One of the kids in the middle of the class had his hand up. He was glancing at his classmates. Janeway recognized the symptoms of a put-up job.

"I suppose it could wait till after class, Admiral," the kid said skittishly.

"As they say in the temporal mechanics department," she encouraged, "there's no time like the present."

The kid turned a few colors and screwed up his daring. "In the year 2377, you aided the Borg resistance movement known as Unimatrix Zero—"

"Sounds like someone's been reading ahead," Barclay commented.

Janeway glanced at him, then looked at the cadet. The kid had moxie, she had to admit that. "I thought you had a question, Cadet."

"Yes, ma'am . . . when you informed the Queen that you were going to liberate thousands of her drones . . . could you describe the look on her face?"

At first she didn't have a clue what that meant. Okay, she still didn't.

Was she missing something?

When in doubt, play smart. She broke a grin and smiled right at the kid as if she knew exactly what he was fishing for.

The cue was right—the other cadets broke into laughter.

Whatever fraternity he was pledging for, he'd probably just guaranteed his membership. Janeway was about to give him extra ballast by actually trying to describe what he asked for, but a Starfleet yeoman drew her attention when he came into the classroom and hurried down the steps toward her. So much for chitchat.

When the yeoman whispered to her and Janeway excused herself from the class, she thought this might be a good lesson too—that speaking to a group of cadets was leisure, not mission, and that even an officer without an assignment had priorities. She left without any more explanation and heard Barclay redirect his students to nanotechnology, but felt his curious eyes tug after her.

They'd all understand, eventually, why her behavior had become so quirkish. Time would tell.

Once in her own office, a cluttered echo of her ready room on *Voyager,* she went immediately to the desk monitor, which was flashing INCOMING MESSAGE: CLASSIFIED.

Classified and time-sensitive. She touched the controls.

Instantly a youthful face replaced the words, a girl in her midtwenties. Miral Paris, the daughter of Tom and B'Elanna.

Janeway pushed down that last part, and forced herself to see a Starfleet ensign instead of practically her own granddaughter.

"Sorry to pull you out of class, Admiral," Miral said quickly.

"Did you see it?" Janeway asked immediately.

"Yes, ma'am."

"And?"

Miral smiled conspiratorially. "It works!"

Janeway allowed herself a deep breath of relief—good news, great news.

"Korath has agreed to the exchange?"

17

Miral's smile fell away. "Yes . . ."

"But?"

"He's insisting on handing it over to you personally."

"I'll be there as soon as I can. Good work, Ensign Paris."

The girl nodded—now, *there* was hero worship.

The monitor blinked to a dark screen and the cryptic conversation ended like a snap. They were engaged in dangerous games, and no mistake, but there was something engaging about all this.

Janeway settled back in her chair. She could easily have resisted, sent a message to Korath that Admiral Janeway didn't just sally off to a Klingon stronghold at his first beckoning. She probably should've toyed with him, led him on, made him believe she wasn't interested in dealing with him or helping him advance his family's influence. He'd have known she was lying and he would've lied back at her and this could've gone on for a while until they were both good and ready to lay things on the line.

No sense dragging out the inevitable. Korath knew what he wanted and Janeway did too. So they'd skip over the general playbook and get right to the end zone.

The reunion was over. Miral had reported in. Korath was primed. Janeway's private shuttle was refitted and ready to fire up. The key pieces were in place. She was thinking clearly and had retired all her doubts long ago.

Just one more obligation.

The day was bright and spectacularly beautiful, as if nature had a proclamation to make. Each time Janeway went outside on such a day, she found herself charged with justification. This, *this,* was why she had driven so hard to come home, this spectacle of Earth, a blue diamond in a sea of stones. Earth was the jewel, the prize, the one planet against which all others constantly paled. Planets all over the cosmos dreamed of being Earth someday. She had been to the Delta Quadrant, farther away than any human had traveled, and she knew how rare such a place was in the greater galactic scheme.

She inhaled the sunlight, the velvety green lawn, and even the magnificent elongated building that seemed to float upon the verdant sea. Well, she was here . . . might as well go inside.

Anticipating the contrast, she steeled herself. These visits were never easy, mostly because they were just visits. There was never progress.

Inside, the hospital made a charming attempt to be as cheerful and uplifting as a long-term medical facility could be, taking every chance to appear less of a hospital. There were potted plants, both real and not, children's paintings, and even a resident collie. The rooms were as homelike as such an arrangement could provide, given that cleanliness was a factor and simplicity helped in that respect. There was personalization without clutter, and the nurses and doctors generally wore street clothes rather than lab jackets. Somehow the effort at *not* appearing to be a hospital tended to ram home the reality of the place. People came here who had nowhere else to go, who needed so much minute-to-minute monitoring that even the most loving of relatives couldn't provide enough attention.

Janeway easily cleared into the place through the residential security. She was a regular.

Without escort she saw herself through the pleasantly curved corridors, through the garden area and into the north wing. Without even thinking she went to the third door on the left and before she knew it she was there. She pressed the coded locking mechanism with her thumb. The mechanism took her fingerprint, bleeped happily, and opened the door panel. She stepped into the near-darkness.

In the room a single candle softly glowed, casting a very faint coloration on the floor, which was patterned with discarded pieces of paper. Hundreds of them. Each piece of paper was crammed with handwriting, numbers, indecipherable encryptions, and carefully executed shapes. There were papers on top of other papers, weeks' worth of frustrated calculations. The candleglow caught the edges of the papers, some curled, some crumpled.

In the middle of the carpet a man's form crouched on both knees, back arched, elbows to the carpet. The furious scratch of a pencil on paper was the only sound in the room.

They'd tried music, but he hadn't liked it. Videos, movies, ship logs, travelogues . . . he'd rejected every attempt to ease his obsessions. All he wanted was the candle, the paper, and a pencil. Not a pen. A pencil.

Janeway stood at the doorway, daylight from the hall windows flooding the entryway.

"Hello, Tuvok."

It was hard to sound normal, casual, not patronizing.

"The light."

"Sorry . . ." She stepped away from the door. The panel closed behind her, locking out the sun, the hope, and any hint of change.

Only now did he look up at her. His Vulcan features were aged, but not so much with time as stress. Unlike the stoic logician he had once been, settled and steady, secure in his identity and purpose aboard *Voyager,* he was easily confused and anxious, his eyes lost, his mouth bracketed with tension.

"I know you . . ." he spoke, disturbing himself with his own voice.

"That's right," Janeway said. "I'm your friend. Kathryn Janeway. Remember?"

His gaze hardened with skepticism. "You're an impostor."

Janeway's stomach knotted up. She'd come here on a final kind of whim, to get the strength to fulfill her plans. It was working.

"No, Tuvok," she insisted. "It's me."

"Admiral Janeway visits on Sunday. Today is Thursday. Logic dictates you are not who you claim to be."

Pleased with his conclusion, Tuvok turned again to whatever he was scrawling on his piece of paper. Well, he had her with that one. This wasn't her usual day, and like a religious tribute she had kept scrupulously to her Sunday visits. Almost everyone else did too, including Tuvok's own family. They had all worked out a specific schedule of visitation and no matter how they felt from day to day, they stuck to their assigned dates and times. Why?

Because Tuvok took his only comfort in regularity, in patterns and dependable, repetitive habit. Spontaneous visits, no matter how enthusiastic, had sent him into fits of panic and weeks of rejection. The only thing that had calmed him down was a set schedule.

"How are you?" she asked.

"I'm close to completing my work," he told her, his eyes on the paper.

So nothing had changed here either.

Janeway sat down in the nearest chair, hoping he might take her cue and stop crouching like a frog on a lily pad. "I'm glad to hear it."

He kept his nose to the paper. "It's difficult with so many interruptions."

"I'm sorry. Would you like me to leave?"

Tuvok contemplated the question as if it were complicated, and made a royal decision. "You may stay."

Janeway watched him for a few seconds. She could indeed have sat here all night and he might not acknowledge her again, having welcomed her into his delusions and accepted her as a fixture. She'd tried that a couple of times—just sit and wait, give him a chance to start a conversation. He never seemed obligated.

The pencil continued to scratch on the paper. The markings were unrecognizable, almost hieroglyphic. From what dark grotto in his disturbed mind had he dredged them?

She wondered if she should ask. Would he tell her?

Would it help?

She had come here today to stiffen her spine, to remind herself of the painful parts of success, of the losses her small family had sustained, and of the failure that everyone else saw as a victory. Her resolve toughened as she sat here, watching one of her best friends sink deeper and deeper into a black lonely pit. If she had any lingering doubts about what she had to do, this visit smashed them.

"Tuvok, there's something I need to tell you," she began. "It's very important."

The pencil continued scratching.

"I'm going away," she continued. "I may not see you again."

At this he surprised her by looking up. Did he understand? Were there thirty seconds of sanity in there for her to make him understand? His dark eyes flickered with the candle's flame as if to say *I must forbid this.*

Janeway forced herself not to expect more.

"Commander Barclay and the Doctor will continue to visit you," she said. "They'll bring you anything you need."

He seemed to be fighting for reason, to respond to the real

problem she had just put before him, but then lost it before he got a good grip. "The Doctor comes on Wednesdays . . . Commander Barclay's visits are erratic."

A frown crossed his face suddenly, sharply. He knew that was the wrong answer, the wrong angle of thought. Like a boy casting a line into rapids, he'd lost the direction of what he was fishing for.

But Kathryn Janeway had gotten what she had come here for.

She stood up quietly, careful not to rustle a single paper with her feet, and moved toward the door.

"Goodbye, Tuvok."

The pencil continued its scratchings. They say to never look back, but she did.

Last-minute second thoughts. She banished them with vigor.

It'd been a long time since she had packed to go away. One trait common to most *Voyager* alumni was the lack of wander-lust.

She laid out a few items of clothing the way she had back in her days of undercover work—the toughest fabrics, the simplest cuts, the least fussy necklines.

"You must be the only doctor who still makes house calls," she commented.

A few steps away, the Doctor produced a medical tricorder and began scanning, but with an attitude.

"What are your symptoms?" he asked.

She looked up. "I'm perfectly fine."

"For thirty-three years, you've fought me every time you were due for a physical. Now you ask me to give you one ahead of schedule?"

He bobbed his brows at her with a you're-sick-or-else delivery.

"I'm taking a trip," she told him. "I just wanted to get our appointment out of the way before I left."

Lies, lies. Had to admit, she was getting better at it.

"That's all?" he prickled.

She managed not to nod. "That's all."

Accommodating what he perfectly well knew was a red herring, he eyed his tricorder and uselessly reported, "The good news is, you're as healthy as the day I first examined you."

"Hm. Well, now that that's out of the way," she said with a gesture, "have a seat. We didn't get to talk much at the party."

"No . . . I suppose we didn't."

"So how's married life?"

Wasn't this silly? She knew, he knew, and still they continued.

"Wonderful," the Doctor accommodated. "You should try it."

She laughed. "I think it's a little late for that."

Thoughts surged back of her long-ago beau, Mark, and those lighthearted days many years ago, just before *Voyager*'s ten-minute mission that had turned into twenty-six years. Funny—she'd thought she was "mature" then, possibly too mature for marriage, for a whole new start, and she had turned Mark down twice. We'll talk about it later . . . don't complicate things . . . let me get this next assignment out of the way, and maybe then . . .

In fact she'd been young in those days, younger than she knew, the captain of a starship with a crew even younger. As she gazed back for just an instant, she recalled how senior and settled they had all believed themselves, as if nothing could go wrong or send them on a fool's mission.

Imagine.

"Marriage is for the young," she said, forcing herself out of her musings. "Like your wife."

"I can only hope," the Doctor commented, "she ages as gracefully as you have. I, of course, will be the same handsome hologram twenty years from now that I am today."

Janeway smiled. What could she possibly say about that? Could she talk about facing life together—at the same pace?

No point. The Doctor was a whole brave new world unto himself. Those troubling details were for his wife to hammer out.

"I've been meaning to ask you," she began again, "are you familiar with the drug called 'chronexaline'?"

A little surprised, the Doctor nodded. He seemed to understand that this was the real reason he had been summoned here by her flimsy cover.

"We've been testing it at Starfleet Medical," he said, "trying to determine if it can protect biomatter from tachyon radiation."

She stopped fiddling with her duffel. "And?"

He looked directly at her. "It's very promising. Why do you ask?"

Ah, the slow dance.

Or a jig. "I need two thousand milligrams by tomorrow afternoon."

This time she really did surprise him.

"Why?" he asked.

"That's classified."

She was asking for his trust, a long-range act of faith, a ridiculously illegal cooperation based on nothing but their mutual past. A few seconds ticked by.

"Will you get it for me?"

"Of course, Admiral. You'll have it by 0900."

He sat on the couch with his hands on his tricorder.

For a moment she thought he might know more than he was

saying, or at least suspect more. Then, as she gazed at him, she realized he was extending that secure chain of trust. She didn't really have any command authority over him anymore. Apparently she didn't need it.

"Thank you," she said. She closed her duffel bag and put it near the door. "I'm taking my private shuttle. Deliver the package to receiving at the Oakland Shipyard. If anyone asks, I'm on vacation."

The Doctor pivoted, still sitting. "Space leave, Admiral?"

She smiled. "Yes, space leave. Take care of Tuvok."

CHAPTER 4

BORG GRAPHICS SCROLLED ACROSS A MONITOR SCREEN AT HIGH speed. Quick glimpses of the Borg cube schematics shot by, ferociously complex and yet recognizable, and suddenly a blend of intersecting warp corridors skated by in patterns of light and mismatched indecipherables.

After hours, the Pathfinder Lab was dimly lit, with only a few worklights on along the walkways between the tiers. Anything more would attract attention from the security scans.

Even after all this time and experience dealing with the Borg, the images rushing past on the screen were processed by Kathryn Janeway's mind more as a recurring nightmare than useful data she was downloading for a purpose.

When the computer shut the screen down and announced, "Download complete," Janeway flinched as if someone had struck her.

"This should be everything you need," Reg Barclay said as he handed her the padd with all the operative information stored neatly inside.

She had no idea what else he might've stored in the device, but suspected there was more than what she had just seen, anything he could think of that might be of use in a clandestine mission.

"The shuttle?" she asked.

"Waiting for you at the Oakland Shipyard," he confirmed. "I wish you'd let me come with you."

"Sorry, Reg, but this is my mission. Besides, if you leave, there won't be anyone to teach those cadets about the Borg."

She was joking. Or was she?

Barclay didn't seem to think so. "I made you some fresh tea for the trip. Not the replicated stuff." He handed her a thermos from under his console desk.

Wasn't this ridiculous? Grown-ups who had known each other for years upon years, gone through times both terrible and glorious, dealt with forces and peoples unknown to any of their kindred, and all they could talk about to each other was tea and who was getting married and frivolous beatings around the bushes. There was more to be said and everyone knew it. They weren't happy. They were home, but they weren't *at home.*

The fractured excuse for conversation galvanized Janeway's sense of purpose and slayed her last lingering doubt. She had to do something, even if it were something crazy.

She took the thermos out of Barclay's hand and rewarded him with a gaze of honesty.

"Thank you," she said, "for everything. I wouldn't have been able to do this without you."

Barclay forced a little smile. "Don't remind me."

* * *

"Any final words of advice for your old captain? Wait—don't tell me. I'm being impulsive. I'm not considering all the consequences. It's too risky."

Anything else? There was more, plenty, all of which she would be saying to anyone else about to go off on this wild quest. As Janeway stared down at the reason for her sudden determination, the wind blew across the grass and fluttered it on Chakotay's name, carved over the dates of his birth and death, on a flat polished piece of marble.

She thought about talking to herself more, using him as an excuse, but instead knelt on the moist grass and touched the stone.

"Thanks for the input, but I've got to do what I think is right." Her voice faltered. She fought to get it back. "I know it wasn't easy living all these years without her, Chakotay . . . but when I'm through, things might be better for all of us. Trust me."

What kind of officer was she? Choked up, doubtful, troubled, alone . . .

The sensation of being alone struck her in the chest. Her long-time first officer was gone, her friends either dead or disengaged from each other, and now she was doing what she had always admonished the others never to do—go off alone, unsupported. How easy it would've been to call Paris, Torres, Doc, and just ask them to come with her, to be a crew again, risk their lives for the sake of . . . their own lives.

No, she couldn't. This was better. This way, if she failed they would still have whatever happiness they had managed to chip out of their return to the Alpha Quadrant.

When she stood, she was once again absolutely sure. Her pledge hung in the air between her and Chakotay, still possessing of its mystery. If she didn't return, at least she wouldn't have to face another reunion.

She turned and walked away from the grave, feeling Chakotay's hands gently push at her back.

"Five-three . . . three-one . . . seven . . . one . . . five-three . . ."

The room was ransacked. The bed was overturned, desk too, papers scattered everywhere, under and above the tumble of sheets and blankets, the splattered candle, a few pathetic personal effects.

"I'm sorry if I pulled you away from something important, sir, but he won't let anyone near him. I thought you might be able to—"

"You did the right thing." *Voyager*'s former ship's doctor gazed down at the crumpled, muttering form of an officer he had once admired for his control and grace under pressure.

Commander Tuvok had once been the steadiest man in the Doctor's limited universe, a kindred spirit of sense and logic, the closest thing a living creature could come to computer perfection—a Vulcan professional aboard a Starfleet ship.

Hardly the picture before the Doctor now.

Tuvok today sat crumpled in a corner of his cubicle here in the Starfleet Medical complex, a sorry echo of his past stability, racked instead by a neurological disease that had simply outpaced the technology to do anything about it.

Both the Doctor and his young colleague, a Starfleet intern in charge of reviewing records on this wing, gazed sorrowfully at the commander. Tuvok still held his rank, thanks to Admiral Janeway's influence. He had, after all, been stricken with this affliction in the line of duty.

Until today Tuvok's behavior had been damningly consistent. He slept fitfully, sometimes with medical assistance, and spent his days insisting upon near-darkness, assuaged by only his single candle, which his family and friends dutifully replenished.

During those days he sifted through his Vulcan mind's tremendous stockpile of knowledge and experience and committed data unendingly to paper with a pencil, also replaced almost daily. What he searched for as he scoured his mind was a mystery. No one had been able to figure out what he was trying to accomplish. No one could help.

"Five-three . . . three-one . . . seven . . . one . . . five-three . . . three-one . . ."

Tuvok's eyes were fixed on an imagined distance. They were focused, sharp, purposeful, not the vacant orbs usually associated with patients who had lost their grip on reality.

Neurological disorders remained among the most complex and confounding of medical troubles. In that, the Doctor could take some comfort. They were doing, and had done, everything within their powers for Tuvok. Until today, there had been neither any changes nor any breakthroughs.

The Doctor was unsure about which of those two he was seeing now.

Beginning at dawn, Tuvok had smashed his room to splinters. He even broke one of the walls.

"His condition's never been associated with violent behavior," the Doctor observed, fishing for confirmations or rumors.

The other physician, a young hotspur who was used to success, had been whittled to worry about this noble Vulcan who couldn't be helped. "He seems more frustrated than violent."

Perhaps the young man was just doing Tuvok a favor, giving him the benefit of the doubt.

"Three-one . . . seven . . . one . . . five-three . . ."

The Doctor made a point to note those numbers and the sequence. Certainly they made some sense, had some bearing, or served as a clue. Even in his least connected moments, Tuvok had always made some glimmer of sense.

He left the intern at the door and moved closer to Tuvok. As he came into the Vulcan's periphery and knew Tuvok could see him, the number recitation suddenly stopped. The Doctor did nothing, but stood still and waited. Tuvok's troubled eyes narrowed as he struggled to think.

"Long-range sensors . . . have detected no trace . . . her disappearance remains a mystery . . . I'm deeply concerned . . ."

The Doctor knelt at his side. "What are you concerned about, Tuvok?"

"Her *disappearance.*"

Tuvok's firm inflection implied that the Doctor should know what he was talking about. So he knew who was in the room with him.

"Whose?" the Doctor asked, cautious not to put any tone to his question.

But once again Tuvok drifted away.

"Five-three . . . three . . . one-seven . . . one . . . five . . ."

Behind them, the young intern said, "He's been repeating those same numbers over and over. Five-three-three-one-seven-one. It might be a stardate . . ."

"Stardate 53317," the Doctor considered. "If my memory files are accurate, that was the day Captain Janeway was abducted by the Kellidians." He gazed at Tuvok and spoke in the most normal, nonpatronizing tone manageable. "Is that who you're talking about? Captain Janeway?"

Tuvok became instantly more agitated, his breath coming quick now, his eyes twitching and troubled. "Her disappearance remains a mystery . . ."

There seemed no solutions to be found here today, and though

Tuvok spoke of mysteries, the Doctor could find none. At least now he knew what Tuvok was trying to remember.

"You solved that mystery, Tuvok," he offered gently. "You rescued the captain and brought her back to *Voyager* safe and sound. Remember?"

"I'm deeply concerned . . ."

The floor creaked and the papers ruffled as the other physician stepped closer. "Maybe if the admiral paid him a visit," he suggested, "showed him she's all right?"

"Unfortunately she's out of town," the Doctor said. "I'm not sure when she'll be back—"

Tuvok's hand shot out and seized him by the arm, dragged him close and held him until they were eye-to-eye.

"She's never coming back!" the Vulcan growled.

The intern jolted and stumbled away toward the door, only to stop himself at the last minute. The Doctor, however, didn't look away from Tuvok's troubled eyes. Something was in there, some clue, some knowledge that *did* apply to today—he was sure of it! They knew each other well enough. Some nodule of reality was trying to force its way from the tangle that had become Tuvok's mind.

As quickly as the lucid moment appeared, it dropped away. Tuvok's hands lost their strength. His eyes went dull again and lost the doctor against the dim roomscape.

"Her disappearance . . . remains a mystery . . ."

The Doctor stood up quickly, before Tuvok became once again disturbed, and stepped out of the Vulcan's periphery. Perhaps it was the vision of himself that had triggered this outburst. Would the same thing happen if Tuvok had seen Paris or any others in the *Voyager*'s crew? He was tempted to experiment, have each surviving member of the command crew visit Tuvok and test this theory.

Haunted by the tidbit of reality he thought he had witnessed in Tuvok's manner, the Doctor stepped past the intern into the hospital corridor. "Record anything he says for the next twenty-four hours. Report to me if there is new data of any kind, anything that is not repeated."

"What does that mean?" Desperate, the intern hustled after him.

"The door," the Doctor reminded.

"Oh! Computer, close and lock compartment 200B."

With a swish the panel closed behind them, sealing Tuvok in with his demons.

The intern hurried to catch up again. "Do you have a procedure in mind? Is there some form of therapy—"

"Not yet. I have to find more information. And I think I know just where to look."

"_Voyager_ to Pathfinder—come in, Pathfinder."

"Doctor!"

The Pathfinder lab was unoccupied, except for its dedicated professor, Mr. Barclay.

The Doctor looked into the lab from the doorway, offering a grin before starting trouble. He could tell as Reg Barclay shot up from his chair and the pile of padds he was working over that Barclay was nervous and expected something like this. The reaction confirmed many suspicions—at least that the suspicions were justified, though still unclear.

"I forgot about our golf game again, didn't I?" Barclay attempted.

"Relax, Reg." The Doctor strode down the aisle to the desk. "It's not until next week." Of course, they both knew this had nothing to do with the golf game. "I'm here because I need to get in touch with Admiral Janeway."

Barclay's lack of a poker face was legendary. "She's out of town."

"I know. Did she tell you where she was going?"

"I'm afraid it . . . never came up. Is something wrong?" Barclay rubbed his hands together.

"I'm not sure. I paid a visit to Tuvok this morning. He had ransacked his quarters in a fit of rage. He's been disturbed, of course, for a long time, but never to this extent, so much that his attending physician deemed it necessary to bring me in immediately. I saw a glint of lucidity during which he seemed to think the admiral is in some sort of danger."

Barclay came around his desk. "You know better than anyone how confused Tuvok can get . . ."

"Yes, but I've been worried about the admiral too."

"Why?"

"Two days ago she asked me for a large quantity of an experimental medication. When I asky why she needed it, she said it was classified."

"Then you shouldn't be telling me about it, should you?"

"I spoke to Director Okaro at Starfleet Intelligence. He assured me that the admiral hasn't been involved in any classified work since she began teaching at the Academy."

Though his hands gave him away by suddenly turning pale, Barclay tried to cover his nervousness with a joke. "You know how sneaky those 'intelligence people' can be. Maybe he was just trying to throw you off."

"Maybe . . . but still . . . she's been talking for months about how excited she is to be teaching with you. Then, just as the semester's starting, she goes away without even telling you where." The Doctor turned and zeroed in on Barclay. "Don't you find that a little troubling?"

"I'm—I'm sure there's—there's a perfectly reasonable explanation," Barclay struggled. "I'm s-sorry, Doctor, but I have
p-paper—papers to grade."

"You're stammering, Reg."

"S-s-s-o?"

With his suspicions confirmed, the Doctor followed Barclay,
who was trying to get away by looping around the other side of
the desk as if he couldn't be found over there.

"I haven't heard you do that in years," he charged. "I think
you *do* know where she is."

Barclay tried not to meet the Doctor's steady eyes. Being a
hologram, the Doctor didn't even have to blink if he didn't want
to and knew he could drill the truth out of the other man with a
good long stare.

"She's one of the most decorated officers in Starfleet history,"
Barclay insisted, his voice shifting higher. "I'm-I'm sure s-s-she
can take c-c-care of herself."

"You wouldn't be saying that unless she was doing something
dangerous!"

Barclay backpedaled as the Doctor followed him around for
the second time. "You're putting words in my mouth . . ."

The Doctor vectored back and met Barclay at a corner. There,
he stopped him with a grip on both arms and a bulletlike glower.
When he spoke, there was no more pretense, no more dancing or
fishing or any other hobby.

For an organized collection of photonic particles, he had a hell
of a grip.

"Tell me where she is, Reg."

CHAPTER 5

A KLINGON FORTRESS ON A CRAGBOUND MOON. THERE WERE A thousand rumors about what these makeshift strongholds really looked like. Even to this modern day, few humans had been allowed the right to pass within such monolithic respositories of survival and tradition. Klingons were volatile and not particularly resourceful, so when they found something that worked and stood the test of time, they stuck with it. Such was the case with rock shelters. They still used them, even though modern construction methods were perfectly available to them.

The moment Kathryn Janeway materialized inside the fortress, she smelled the telltale odor of synthetic rock. Apparently Korath wasn't so stuck in tradition that he was beyond making use of some modern conveniences. Synthetic silk, synthetic ivory—why not synthetic stone?

Torchlight confused her eyes briefly, compounded by the whine of transporter beams, which always set Janeway's teeth on edge. Though she didn't have to, she usually held her breath during transporting. No idea why. Just a reaction, slightly troubled by the idea of leaving her shuttle on autopilot in orbit. The vehicle was secured by code and every other available trickery, but she still found herself wishing there were a living accomplice up there, just in case.

The moon had no atmosphere, which meant this place had to be airtight and secure—another good reason to go technical. The scent of artifice gave her a thrill of confidence. She could understand this manner of living. The image of the primitive was fake, and probably shored up by plenty of mechanics to stabilize everything from life support to aesthetics. She could work with that.

Before her as the fortress came into form she made out the dim figures of two Klingons—easy enough to identify just by the torchlight-backed silhouettes—and the smaller, less-armored form of Miral Paris between them.

Beyond them was a corridor of jagged stone lit by wall torches. The effect was decidedly medieval, yet the stones had an artificial sparkle and gloss along their edges.

"Welcome to the House of Korath, admiral," Miral said, speaking firmly and loudly, to establish beyond doubt that Janeway was to be accepted here.

"I love what he's done with the place." Janeway's voice echoed.

The Klingon to Miral's left suddenly erupted, *"Guv'ha gor! Nu'Tuq mal!"*

Miral snapped to him and barked, *"P'Tak! Gaht bek'cha tuq mal gun'mok!"*

The Klingon fixed his hands into a set of claws at his sides, but otherwise made no other threats. Miral skewered him to some silent promise, then approached Janeway without either of the guards.

"What was that about?" Janeway asked. She had picked up a couple of words, though the delivery said more.

In the torchlight, Miral's one-quarter of Klingon blood seemed to show more in the soft brow ridge on her forehead than it did in ordinary light. Or perhaps the effect of this place was simply working on Janeway's imagination.

"He said your demeanor was disrespectful."

Janeway glanced at the Klingons. "I hope you told him I didn't mean to be rude."

"I told him if he didn't show *you* more respect, I'd break his arm."

With a little chuckle of admiration, Janeway shook her head. "You're your mother's daughter."

Miral beamed, but managed not to smile. That might've been taken by the Klingons as a sign of weakness at this juncture. "Korath's waiting. We should go in."

So much for small talk.

The girl started to lead the way through the caverns, but Janeway put out a hand. "Sorry, but this is where we part ways."

"Excuse me?"

"You're dismissed, Ensign."

"Admiral, I really think—"

"I can take care of myself."

Miral pivoted to face her. "With all due respect, I've been working on this for six months!"

"And you've done an exemplary job. But it's over. Understand?"

Miral Paris had grown up on the decks of a starship, aboard which Kathryn Janeway was the captain, the all-powerful benevolent dictator who kept their small segment of the universe safe and even on its keel. All things had to be approved by the captain. All problems lay at the captain's feet, all dangers and threats kept at bay by the captain's resolve. There was nothing short of hero worship in the girl's eyes now, coupled soundly with a desire to gain the approval and trust of this monumental paragon before her.

She still wanted to go.

"Yes, ma'am," she said anyway.

Janeway couldn't help but empathize. Passings of the torch were sometimes hard to swallow for those doing the passing, especially when the torch went to a higher authority who hadn't done the footwork. The girl had done her job, better than most and with fewer questions. Possessiveness over an assignment was one of those things Starfleet encouraged, and generally it went along with plain old human nature—and Klingon nature. Miral had all that going for her. She wanted to finish what she had started.

But Kathryn Janeway had set herself upon this course single-handed and she meant to finish it alone. All these other untidy ends had to be shunted aside. She could be considerate later, if things worked out.

"I happen to know your parents are anxious to spend some time with you," she suggested, being deliberately vague and even condescending. If Miral resented this enough, the girl would get off this rock and take herself out of the equation as a possible target or hostage. "Take a few days' leave," Janeway added. "Go and see them."

Few people truly understood the tenuous nature of dealings with Klingons more than those with Klingon blood, Klingon rage surging through their veins, however removed. The surge of temper, of passions and determinations; involuntary drives of single-mindedness were sometimes indescribable. Miral Paris, unlike her mother, B'Elanna, rather embraced the mystique of her ancestry, but that was because she had never really lived among Klingons, but only dabbled in the idea. For her this was still adventure and not a way of life. She was a Starfleet ensign on an undercover assignment. Her ability to speak Klingon without a hint of accent, another gift of genetics, had been an advantage, and even more, Janeway had wanted to give this girl a chance to prove herself as more than just a daughter of the famous *Voyager* crew, just a survivor along for the ride. Everybody deserved that.

Miral swallowed whatever insult she found in the admiral's dismissal of her at this critical moment, and with fierce self-control she simply nodded and gestured the admiral down the correct corridor.

There, in the torchlit cavern, Janeway left what she hoped would be the last of her "clan" involved in this new trick.

The corridors were long, curved, and arid. The air was perfumed, but circulating and cool. Led by the Klingon guards, Janeway passed by several untidy antechambers. She saw no one else moving around.

Ultimately they turned left, and left again into a larger room with poor lighting, cluttered with incongruous pieces of machinery, some recognizable, others alien contraband. At the center of this jagged junk heap was Korath.

For a species that considered themselves rebellious, the Klingons did all they possibly could to look alike. Korath was as typical an old-man Klingon as any Janeway had ever seen. He seemed to be going for clichéd image—the long gray hair, uncombed, the exaggerated brow ridge that got more prominent as Klingons aged, the unnecessary body armor and uncomfortable clothing, the sour attitude. He was working on some kind of laser tool to adjust a hand weapon that Janeway didn't recognize.

The two Klingon guards paused at the entryway. Janeway continued into the lab as if she visited every day.

Korath knew she was here, but kept working on his toy. After a few moments of time-wasting, he turned the tool off and held up the weapon.

"A Cardassian disruptor," he boasted. "I've modified it to emit a nadion pulse."

Fine. Can it knit and purl?

"Impressive," Janeway bothered to say, unable to think of anything more original. "But that's not what I've come for."

"No. You've come for something far more dangerous."

In no hurry, he picked up another tool and went on tinkering with his disruptor. If he thought he was really impressing anybody, he'd been in these caves way too long.

"Where is it?" Janeway demanded. All the deals had been dealt. Why was he stalling?

"Somewhere safe," he grumbled.

Oh, brother. Pseudo-superiority. Did he have to be so bracingly predictable?

Janeway decided to play the uninspired game for a minute or two. "I went to a great deal of trouble to get you your seat on the High Council. Now give me what you promised."

Korath moved to a monitor embedded in the fake rock of the cavern wall and activated it. A rotating graphic of Janeway's personal shuttle, the one in orbit right over their heads, popped on. A little grainy, but accurate enough. At the side of the screen, Klingon text scrolled ceaselessly.

"I've scanned your shuttle. You've made some interesting modifications."

He hit a button, and the graphics zoomed in on a single component.

"Your shield generator is of particular interest," he concluded.

Janeway watched the monitor with a little more pride than she had practiced. "It's not for sale."

Korath smiled craggily. "Then what you want isn't available either."

"We had an agreement."

The old Klingon made a gesture to the two guards and without much theatricality said, "Show the admiral out."

She strode back into Korath's throne room and announced, "I've reconsidered your offer."

"I thought you might," he said.

"I'll give you the shield emitter," she continued, as if he'd said nothing at all, "but not until I've inspected the device you're offering. To make sure it's genuine."

Korath's dark face flushed purple. "You question my honor?"

"No," she said. "If you had any honor, you wouldn't have changed the terms of our agreement. Show it to me or I'm leaving."

Her ultimatum was so matter-of-fact that Korath seemed to believe her. She half believed it herself.

Janeway held her arms and legs very still. Klingons might take any twitch as a signal that they had some advantage, psychological or otherwise, or perhaps even judge any movement as tension. They might interpret unease in any of a dozen ways that would work against her. She fixed her eyes on Korath and focused her whole physical self to a single end. The two guards might as well have been stone carvings, for all the attention she offered them.

A large section of the rock wall shimmered and frizzled out of existence—a holographic projection. When the picture of rock went away, the chasm revealed a storage locker. Inside the locker was a table, and on that table was a temporal deflector.

Until now, she had held in store an idea that the temporal deflection science was a myth running around between the raggedy Empire and the Federation and a few other concerns about a device that could do what this one supposedly could do. Miral had said it worked, but young idealistic ensigns could be deluded. They wanted so much to believe . . .

If it could do what the rumors said, why was its price as low as a seat on the Klingon Council?

Then, there was no accounting for taste—or ceilings on ambition. Some people just wanted to get the best of their mothers-in-law. Korath wanted to be able to look down on all the other Klingons from the only pinnacle that meant anything to him.

The deflector's casing was more aerodynamic than Janeway had imagined, built with more artistry than necessary. The streamlined device would fit well on her shuttle. She could already see the way to fit it on and connect it to a power source.

She pulled her tricorder around from where it had rested on its strap under her arm and activated it. Casual, casual.

With strict inner control she said nothing, but went about analyzing the device like a good science officer indulging a bit of curiosity. Everybody deserved a little confirmation now and then. Korath didn't stop her. If she had explained, he might have grown suspicious. So far she wasn't doing anything unexpected, other than possibly moving too close to the device.

Six steps . . . five . . . she had to be within range, no margin of error.

Why was he dumb enough to let her get so close? Ah, the small favors of life and luck.

Korath moved closer too, watching her every move, listening to the twitter of the tricorder, measuring just how much information was enough. He had his Cardassian disruptor in his hand. Janeway hadn't missed that little detail.

She had no weapon of her own. The fortress's shields would never have let her beam through with a sidearm. All she had was the tricorder and its merry scan.

Which was good enough for now. She looked up at Korath. "This'll do just fine."

Like a cat batting a toy, she slapped the deflector device on the midsection of its casing, leaving behind a small magnetic transporter enhancer. With the other hand she thumbed the control plate of her tricorder with a predetermined code, then held her breath. The air around her began to whine.

Both she and the deflector began to dematerialize.

"Stop her!" Korath's shout echoed through the caverns. He raised his disruptor.

The two Klingon guards pulled their weapons also and opened fire.

Janeway hunched her shoulders. The heat of weapons fire crawled across her skin. Whether the transporter would operate fast enough or the disruptor fire would cut through the beams first, she couldn't calculate.

As for Korath and their deal, she had already paid in full.

CHAPTER 6

"COMPUTER, DEPLOY ARMOR."

Janeway gave her shuttle its marching order before she had completely materialized in the cockpit. The shuttle hummed with a surge of power, and began to enjoy a *pokpokpok* sound as plate armor unfolded in successive shingles across the outer hull. What a terrific sound. The benefits of dealing with aliens in far-flung corners. Still a few tricks up her sleeve.

Without taking the time to enjoy her advantage, she stepped to the nav board and tapped in the numbers. "Lay in a course for these coordinates—"

The shuttle rocked hard to port and almost knocked her down. The Klingons here already? Korath had more influence than he thought. Of course, she'd just put him on the High Council, which hadn't hurt his ability to muster firepower.

Janeway glanced at the armor readouts—holding. Good stuff. Just to be annoying, she tapped the trigger for the incoming comm receiver. Korath's image flickered on a monitor, transmitting from his rock cave.

"What do you want?" Janeway asked

"You'll pay for your deceit, ghuy' cha! *The House of Korath won't rest until you've been drowned in your own blood—"*

"I'd love to stay and chat, but I'm on a tight schedule."

She hit the control that cut him off and the monitor snapped dark. Oh, that was fun!

"Computer, warp six," she added. Time to get down to business.

Double-crossers like Korath were always easy targets. She had dealt with so many aliens and such varied psychologies in the Delta Quadrant that handling Klingons was a picnic.

As easily as that, she left Korath and his insulted ego behind.

She settled into her pilot seat and forced herself to relax, a trick she had practiced from long ago. A shuttle at warp six wasn't like a starship speeding along. There weren't twelve decks between her and space, no heavily insulated cushioning, no superstructure to absorb the effects of speed impossible in nature. Here, in this shuttle with its skin of alien armor, she could feel the warping of space upon her skin and in her muscles, behind her eyes and on the back of her neck.

Suddenly she thought of Chakotay. He could never feel it. He always said it was her imagination, that she couldn't really wake up out of a sound sleep and know whether or not the ship had gone to warp speed.

She had that sensation now, felt the thrill of high science racing across the tiny hairs on her arms. Even a hothead like Korath knew better than to chase her, and if he did the armor would confound him. But he wouldn't.

Had Miral cleared the moon and made good on her escape?

If I were all that sure of myself, I wouldn't worry.

"Approaching designated coordinates," the computer informed placidly.

Janeway sat up quickly. "All stop."

"Warning: vessel approaching, vector one-two-one mark six."

She leaned forward and confirmed the sensor reading. Who would be out here?

Other kinds of alarms went off in her head. Had she failed to keep her plans completely to herself? To keep all the secrets? She and her crew had become deeply skilled at reading each other's silences—had she involuntarily given herself away to them?

"Oh . . . damn," she murmured as the hail came through. "I knew things were going too well . . . computer, retract armor."

Pokpokpokpokpok—the shuttle drew in its alien shingles.

Through her forward viewport, Janeway peered at a starship, one of the newly commissioned line, huge as it hung over the shuttle. On the comm monitor, a family face appeared.

Janeway sighed. "Harry . . . and people are always saying space is so big."

"Lower your shields, Admiral," Kim ordered, *"and stand by for transport. I'm taking you into custody."*

"You have no grounds for taking me into custody, Captain," she told him.

He really didn't. All she'd actually done was take a drive in her personal shuttlecraft. Nobody else knew about Korath, and that wasn't Federation jurisdiction anyway. What was he going to do, arrest her for skipping class?

Harry still had a boyishness about him despite the passing of years, and he didn't like doing what he was about to do. She could see that in his eyes, and in his hesitation.

"Reg told the Doctor everything," he said. *"And the Doctor told me."*

"You'd think I'd have earned their loyalty after all these years," Janeway complained, not without a grain of truth.

"They care about you too much to let you do this. And so do I."

Janeway held up her hand before he made a direct command to anyone on his bridge and had her beamed aboard. "On one condition—you let me explain why I'm doing this."

"Done. Prepare to beam over."

Janeway hardly had time to walk into Harry's—Captain Kim's—ready room when he laid into her. *"Chronexaline? A Klingon temporal deflector? Miral Paris in Klingon territory at your order . . . Chakotay's funeral, the tenth reunion . . . Admiral, it doesn't take a sixth-grade graduate to figure out what you have in mind. You have no idea what the consequences would be!"*

"I know what the consequences are if we do nothing," Admiral Janeway said. "So do you." Suddenly empassioned, she leaned forward. "I have a chance to change all that!"

"If Starfleet command knew what you were trying to do—" Kim cut himself off.

Janeway took a moment to glance around Kim's ready room. A Kal-Toh game, a few photographs, and a weathered hockey stick showed her that while Harry might be a captain now, he was still in part the young man she had know so many years ago. "You haven't told them?"

"The Doctor and I decided to keep things in the family."

She understood his problem from both sides. He was a Starfleet captain now, sworn not to do the bidding of his former captain, or even to look after the well-being of shipmates past and present, but to oversee the welfare of the entire Federation. His job was not to consider how the past had mutilated the present, but to defend the present as it had become.

Yes, what she had in mind was a fabulous risk. Everybody in Starfleet knew how touchy these experimental missions could be. But they had been executed before and had worked out—if you could believe the logs of heroes and dreamers . . .

"What about your crew?" she asked. After all, he had a new "family" now.

"I told them I needed to take you back to Starfleet medical because you'd contracted a rare disease."

She smiled. "I hope it's not terminal."

"No," he said. *"But it's been known to affect judgment."*

"I know what I'm doing, Harry."

"Do you? Can you say with absolute certainty that it'll work? Because if you can't . . . even if it weren't a violation of every rule in the book, it would still be far too risky."

Well, that was the obligatory argument, the one he must make by rote, the most obvious and clichéd of scoldings. At least it was out of the way. Risk had never been their problem. They had eaten it for breakfast, lunch, and dinner every other day. None of the *Voyager* crew would be put off by such a claim anymore. Risk? Who was he kidding?

She found herself smiling at him. As he watched her expression, he started to twitch.

"What?" he asked.

"Oh, I'm . . . remembering a young ensign who wanted to fly into a Borg-infested nebula, just to explore the remote possibility that we might find a way home . . ."

"If I remember correctly," he pointed out, *"you stopped me."*

She nodded, caught in her own strictures. "We didn't know then what we know now."

"Our technology might have improved, but—"

"I'm not talking about technology. I'm talking about people. People who weren't as lucky as you and I."

He was starting to waver. Janeway could read his expression. Harry Kim had no poker face at all. He might be a starship captain, but when he found himself dealing with the woman who had been *his* captain for virtually his entire life—well, he hadn't been in that command chair long enough to cancel out the schoolteacher effect.

And there was more . . . he knew that she would be doing the same thing if he were one of the unfortunate among them. Their losses were so random, their dissatisfactions so deeply seated, he could hardly ignore the purity of her reasons for doing what she planned. Yes, there were hazards, but there always had been. Harry wasn't here to protect the whole Federation against a well-established risk factor. He was here to protect a member of his family from stepping into the busy street from which they had so barely escaped.

She could use that. None of them were happy enough in their lives here to justify his stopping her.

"You said," she began, "that you and the Doctor wanted to keep things in the family. But our family's not complete anymore, is it?" A few seconds passed as she let her words work on him, and all her silent thoughts pass between them without overtalking the things they both knew. "I'm asking you to trust my judgment, Harry . . . one last time."

His expressive eyes crinkled a little. Janeway doubted that anyone on his bridge would even notice.

"I'll do better than that," he said. *"I'll help you."*

* * *

Once he had made such a decision, he stuck to it. There were no more doubts or clichés running behind his expression when he beamed over to her shuttle. Together, without taking the added help of any of Harry's crew, they wrestled the deflector into position on top of the shuttlecraft and jury-rigged it into place, then fixed it to the shuttle's appropriate power streams. They spoke no more of risks.

"If Starfleet Command finds out I had anything to do with this, they'll demote me back to ensign," Kim commented when they were back inside the shuttle and at work on the interior modifications.

An ironic comment, considering everything.

"You worry too much, Harry," Janeway told him. "It's turning you gray."

"This device of Korath's, it produces too much tachyo-kinetic energy. It could burn itself out by the time you get where you're going." He looked away from the monitor that was giving him this information and added, "You wouldn't be able to get back."

"I always assumed it was a one-way trip."

She was at peace with her decision, but Harry's face was still pale with concern. He didn't point out any other drawbacks or suspicions about the technology, or that Korath could have this all completely wrong and this thing on the outer hull might be a very fancy washing machine indeed—or tissue scrambler, whichever came first. Like the first experiments with transporters, she could be betting her life on neo-voodoo.

"Ready for the last-minute flight check?" he asked.

"Go ahead."

"Cue monitor four."

A rotating graphic of the shuttle popped on, complete with the temporal device mounted on the hull like a hat on a rabbit.

"You're sure I can't talk you out of this," Harry mentioned, then answered his own query. "Right . . . stupid question."

He stood up, turned to her, and she gathered him into her arms. The concept of command fell away. They were two close relatives saying farewell, no uniforms, no rank.

She broke the embrace before they were both plunged again into the whole picture of what this might become.

Harry stepped back and tapped his combadge. "Kim to the *Rhode Island*. One to beam back."

The *Rhode Island* made good on its captain's promise and warped out almost immediately. No witnesses. Harry couldn't be faulted for failing to log something he hadn't seen or traces his scanners never read.

Again Janeway was alone. She had toyed with the idea that maybe she wouldn't feel quite so isolated now that Harry Kim was on her side, and knowing the Doctor and Reg were with her in spirit.

Didn't work. She was by herself, with her own commitment, and she felt every moment go by with a pinch.

Still, she couldn't shake the very real sensation of holding all their lives in her hands. She didn't really want to shake that feeling—it was very real.

At least she didn't have to talk anybody else into letting her follow through, didn't have to trick any more Klingons or endanger any more ensigns. Now she had only to speak to the computer on her shuttle, and it would follow her every command to the smallest degree.

"Computer," she began, and drew a long breath, "activate the chrono-deflector."

A low hum with a two-note harmony vibrated through the

shuttle's hull, growing in depth and volume. The power-source connection was solid. Now, if only the device didn't spin her into the tenth century B.C.—

"Warning," the computer spoke. "Ship approach, mark four-two."

"Now what?" Janeway punched the controls. "Identify!"

But the computer never got a chance. Two gull-winged cruisers decloaked in near space and opened fire.

Klingons!

CHAPTER 7

THE KLINGONS ROARED IN BLAZING. NO TALK, NO THREATS, NO deals.

"Deploy armor!" Janeway shouted over the scratch of disruptor fire.

"Unable to comply. Ablative generator is off-line."

Boom—the shuttle rocked again.

"Evasive pattern beta-six!"

The autonav system flared to life and the roller-coaster ride began. Janeway would've been thrown to her knees if she hadn't known which direction the shuttle would veer first.

"Open a channel to the *Rhode Island!*"

The comm bleeped, and a picture of Harry Kim appeared on the comm monitor. Before he had a chance to ask why she had hailed him, Janeway said, "Harry, I'm under attack. How fast can you get back here?"

"Two minutes, tops. Full about!"

"Acknowledged. I can hold on for two minutes. Evasive pattern alpha-z!"

The shuttle took a nosedive. Two Klingon disruptor streams crossed in space and mutually detonated, rocking Janeway with ambient energy, but otherwise missing her. She made a bet with herself and duplicated the move on the starboard vector.

Sure enough, the Klingons tried again to triangulate on her and ended up blasting each other's disruptor streams. The shuttle rattled, but burst through clean. The computer didn't even report any damage.

Twice more in a row, for nearly a whole minute, she was able to cause the Klingons to completely waste their shots before they realized what she was doing. Once they almost raked each other wing to wing. After the near-collision, they paused firing for a few moments, trying to get her into their scopes without boxing each other in.

She took those moments to tap the comm system.

"Well, Korath, when you hold a grudge, you really hold it high, don't you?"

"Surrender, cheat!"

"I didn't cheat you," she said. "I gambled and won, that's all. I'm sure you know the type of game we're in together. Sometimes we have to play through, or no one wins."

Stall, stall . . .

"You stole my device!"

"I'm no thief. All I did was bruise your pride. You have your payment in full. You would never have attained the position you have now if not for my influence. Your price was a high one for a Starfleet officer. It cost me a piece of my reputation."

"I have reputation to protect as well, Janeway. You and your alien science make a threat to my people. As a member of the High Council, it is my—"

"Oh, you've got to be kidding," she drawled. "I've heard of

tortured logic before, but spare me this shadow of nobility! You're on the High Council, so you have to protect your people against me, who put you there? You missed your calling, Korath. You should've become a song-and-dance man."

"Klingons do not dance."

As long as he was talking, he wasn't shooting. The other ship made a few shots as Janeway's shuttle swerved and plunged, but without Korath's lead ship giving it a fighting pattern, the second vessel had no cue to take. He obviously wasn't a skilled battle leader, or he wouldn't have been so easily distracted.

The shuttle was smaller than either of the two Klingon ships, and far more maneuverable in a tight area. Janeway disengaged the autonav and took the pilot controls herself with one hand, while with the other hand she recalibrated the generator and found power for the temporal deflector. She piloted a spiral pattern, stressful enough for the narrow-bodied shuttle, almost impossible for the Klingons.

Whoever was in charge of the second Klingon ship was smarter or maybe just more experienced than Korath. The second ship anticipated her next two moves and opened fire. When she came out of her spiral, she ran straight through the disruptor stream.

Deadly energy crackled across the shuttle's hull amidships and across the port flank. Only by turning up on her quarter at the last instant did Janeway protect the precious device affixed to the shuttle's upper hull. Sparks erupted inside the cockpit, both before and behind Janeway. She was suddenly working in a sea of smoke and heat. The controls began breaking down under her fingers; the shuttle began to shake uncontrollably.

"Stabilize, stabilize," she mumbled, but nothing worked. The shuttle couldn't regain steadiness.

"This is the Starship Rhode Island. *Stand down your hostile action or we will open fire."*

"Harry! A little early, too. Very nice." Janeway leaned into the controls and increased speed to get the shuttle out of the way as the starship swooped back into firing range.

The shuttle was cracking in half. She could feel it losing its grip, hissing atmosphere into space, grinding against its own bones as the systems tried to keep their bloodlines going.

In her periphery as she fought to keep her shuttle together, she saw the *Rhode Island* plunge into the scene and bite at the heels of both Klingon ships without breaking a sweat. The two ships split formation and raced into wide evasive maneuvers, but didn't leave the area.

"Stand by for transport, Admiral," Harry's voice ordered.

Janeway glanced at the comm monitor—yes, there he was.

"You know where I'm going, Harry, and it's not to your ship."

"Your structural integrity is failing."

"Just get these Klingons off my tail."

The starship instantly veered out of transporter range and blasted fiercely at one of the Klingons, effectively disabling the baddies with a bitter strafe. As the Klingon went streaming off on a crooked trail, *Rhode Island* roared after the second while Janeway coaxed her shuttle to hold together and still find the power to charge the deflector. Now she could afford to pay attention to what she was doing and forget about Korath and associates.

"Computer, activate the tachyon pulse and direct it to these spatial and temporal coordinates."

Temporal coordinates—dangerous words.

Space began to stretch and blur before her. From over her head, a wide-angle pulse shot out from the deflector and created a cut in space, a broad wound in the universe.

ENDGAME

Janeway aimed her shuttle, damage and cracks and all, toward that crack and leaned on the impulse speed until there was no going back, until not even the braking thrusters could veer her off her course.

Above her head the temporal deflector hummed and pulsed its beacon into the wound, black on blacker. The great mouth of space opened and gulped her down.

CHAPTER 8

Starship Voyager
The Delta Quadrant
Twenty-six years earlier

SOMETIMES HE DREAMED OF DRIVING THE SHIP. THE IDEA THAT anybody else could do it the way the ship liked . . . surge up on those solar winds and skid down the weak side . . . read the spectral shifts and avoid the rough spots . . . it wasn't what people thought. Still, he wished the ship had a yoke or a wheel, the real thing, to let him feel the movements through his hands the way he could in the holograms of early flight—you could really *lean* into a plane in those days, or a motorcycle or a bike—so why couldn't a starship have a joystick?

"Tom."

Of course, nobody else knew about the skid traction trick. He'd invented that himself, and never told anybody. Okay, so it was a little egotistical, even rotten. Didn't hurt anything. Everybody had their little tricks, ways to do their own jobs that made them look better than anybody else. There—solar flares from a blue giant. The best kind!

"*Tom.*"

"I'm 'sleep."

"It's time."

"Mmmm . . . for what?"

"I'll give you one guess."

Were the lights on? Why would she put the lights on in the middle of off-watch?

Tom Paris's eyes popped open as his brain crawled out of the navigation dream and suddenly hit high speed. He almost fell off the bed—almost right out of his T-shirt.

Beside him, B'Elanna was sitting up in bed as best she could, her eyes serious and wide as she contemplated her once-svelte body, looking very much as if she'd swallowed a pumpkin.

Paris felt his back muscles scream as he jolted up and slapped his chest, looking for his combadge. "Paris to—Paris to—"

Where was it? On the nightstand!

"Paris to sickbay! It's time!"

Over the system the Doctor's voice was annoyingly arid. "*Remain calm, Mr. Paris. Can she stand?*"

"Uh—I—uh—" He found his feet and turned to ask her, but she was already up and putting on her robe. Extra-large.

"Affirmative," Paris said into the combadge.

"*Then I suggest you report to sickbay.*"

"What about B'Elanna?"

"*Her too.*"

She was already heading for the door as he dragged his own robe off the floor. "Maybe we should use the transporter—wait for me!"

B'Elanna was taking small shuffling steps, but moving right

along at a quick enough pace that Paris had to step lively to keep up.

"Don't you think we should—"

"I can walk. I'm pregnant, not crippled."

She sounded mad. Was she supposed to sound mad? Who was she mad at?

Uh-oh.

"Can I—is there anything—"

"No, Tom, you've already done *everything* you could possibly do to me. Sorry—*for* me."

"Aw, come on," he implored, daring to take her elbow. "You wanted this, didn't you? It's a little late to change your mind, isn't it?"

"I haven't changed my mind. I don't want to be pregnant anymore. I can't eat, I can't breathe, I can't walk, I can't fight, and I feel like a damned Trill. And don't touch me."

For somebody who couldn't breathe, she was doing a good job talking. Not touching her was hard—he wanted to help, guide, lead—*something*. All she would let him do was open the turbolift a second before she got there so she didn't have to break her stride.

Two decks seemed like twenty. Then came the long corridor to sickbay. Paris felt as if they were crossing a tundra.

The Doctor was saucily stoic as Paris more or less herded B'Elanna into sickbay. "Right here, please," he said, indicating his favorite diagnostic couch. "So, Miss Torres, you believe you're ready to deliver this parcel?"

"I'm ready," she said on a little gasp. "I'm beyond ready. I'm—"

"No talking, please." As B'Elanna struggled to lie back on the clamshell, the Doctor studied her from shoulders to knees with his medical scanner and was done damnably fast.

"Well?" Paris urged. "Any minute now, right? Can you hurry it up somehow?"

The Doctor ignored him and doubled his scan. Finally he clicked the device off and cryptically said, "You're going to have a very healthy baby. But not tonight."

"Tell me you're joking!" B'Elanna grumped.

"You're experiencing false labor, Lieutenant."

"Again?" Paris blurted.

"As I explained the last time, it's a common occurrence, especially among Klingons—"

B'Elanna struck the sides of the couch with her sharp fists. "I want this thing out of me!"

"Misdirected rage," the Doctor commented. "Another common occurrence among Klingons."

Paris felt as if his face were about to fall off. He rubbed it and moaned, "Can't you induce?"

"I wouldn't recommend it."

"If this keeps happening, we'll never get any sleep."

"You think it's bad now?"

Paris exchanged a contemplative gaze with his wife, who looked every bit as dismayed as angry. Well, she could be as angry as she wanted to, couldn't she? This one little person was the only creature in the galaxy who didn't particularly care how much she ranted. The baby was in charge.

Captain Janeway was glad of the interruption when Chakotay streamed into her ready room and rescued her from having to scan the power ratio reports from belowdecks. During these long periods of busy work—which really did have to be done for the sakes of preparedness and conservation—she always tried to remind herself that the boring times in space were offset by truly dangerous and ghastly adventures. Still, during one she often craved the other.

"It happened again," Chakotay mentioned right off. His strong features and gentle charming eyes brightened the ready room and set off a competition between stars passing outside the viewport.

Janeway stretched back and smiled. "That baby's leading us on. When did it happen?"

"Oh four hundred."

She winced in empathy for Paris and B'Elanna. Another night's sleep ruined. "How many false alarms does this make?"

"Three. That we know of."

"That baby's as stubborn as her mother."

Chakotay smiled. "Harry's starting a pool to see who can guess the actual date and time of birth."

"Tell him to put me down for next Friday, twenty-three hundred hours. Anything else?"

Chakotay shrugged lightly, every bit as bored as she was. Technically he was in command now, and he almost never bothered her during her off-watch hours for anything other than two good reasons—acute danger to the ship, or acute boredom for the first officer.

"Crewman Chell's asked about taking over in the mess hall full time."

Whew—they really were scraping the bottom of the barrel. A flash of reality struck Janeway that on a ship of the line, the captain and first officer would never even hear about who was handling the mess hall. The whole structure of running a ship simply prevented the minute details of life belowdecks from filtering up so high. This was more like silly gossip than a problem for command officers.

True, the ship's cook could make or break the quality of life belowdecks, especially in a near-survival situation, and could keep the crew going, but this just wasn't the kind of thing she should have to be discussing with her first officer.

Janeway threw it a bone anyway. "Neelix left some pretty big pots to fill. Does Mr. Chell think he's up to the challenge?"

"Apparently so," Chakotay said casually, and handed her a padd. "He prepared a sample menu."

Janeway scanned the information and crinkled her nose. "Plasma leek soup? Chicken warp-core-don-bleu?"

"If his cooking's as bad as his puns, we're in trouble."

"Oh, I don't know . . . I wouldn't mind giving his red-alert chili a try . . . feel like having lunch?"

"I'd love to. But I already have plans. Rain check?"

"Absolutely." He turned and headed for the door, which in fact opened at his approach before he changed his mind and peered at her over his shoulder.

Janeway felt his gaze even though she had gone back to the work on her desk. When she didn't hear the door close, she looked up. "What's wrong?"

"Yes. What's wrong with you?"

"Psychic, are we, Chakotay?"

He strode back toward the desk and pressed one finger to the black surface. "You've been more nervous than Tom. You're not giving birth to this baby, you know. It's Tom and B'Elanna's problem."

"Is it?" She drew a long breath. "I thought I'd put my misgivings to rest."

"Kathryn, you can't stop them from starting families. It's one way they feel less captive."

In a kind of annoyed fitfulness, Janeway pulled her fingers through her hair and tried to relax. "A long time ago, I came to a decision that there would be no children on *Voyager.* Remember?"

"I do remember. You suffered over that decision. And if memory serves, it was just a few months before Naomi was born."

She nodded at the irony. "Yes, it was one of those brilliant command decisions that lasted about six seconds before I had to swallow it."

"The only other option is find a planet, park the ship and plant a colony, and start our lives over there. The idea has come up before."

Janeway's chair squeaked under her as she pivoted and put one foot up on the leg of her desk. She fixed her eyes on the part of the wall where the viewport met the bulkhead and got very interested in the seam. "I've been over and over this. *Voyager* is a Starfleet ship on a mission. It's not our ship . . . it belongs to the people of the Federation. They built it, supported it, educated all of us and sent us into space with this fabulous resource . . . it's our sworn duty to return this vessel and its power back into their hands.

"Our priority is to return this ship and its strength and all we know about the Borg to the Federation so we can mount a singular plan to deal with them. That's our mission. Our *only* mission." She stood up and stretched her legs—how long had she been sitting? "If we forget that, we're just the passengers on some vague journey whose end we can't plot out."

"No one's forgetting that," Chakotay pointed out. "No captain in Starfleet has ever had to command the kind of ship you have here or this kind of mission. We only brought half the 'the book' to the Delta Quadrant with us."

"Seven years, Chakotay . . ." Janeway murmured. "Two years longer than the usual deep-space mission, and those are usually punctuated with home leave from time to time. And our mission wasn't a long one anyway. They crew was expecting to go home after a few months at the longest. Paris didn't even know B'Elanna. Tuvok has a wife and five children. Five! You and I were on opposite sides of a local conflict . . . my setter had had puppies . . ."

"I think we can forgive ourselves for improvisation, don't you?" he suggested. "You're mourning the fact that we've been lost for seven years. How about giving ourselves credit for having survived seven years when we didn't in any way intend to be out so long? Most ships are provisioned for months before a voyage like this. We've actually learned to be comfortable."

"Too comfortable," Janeway complained. "Naomi was one thing; an entire second generation, growing up on this ship, makes me very conscious of the time that's passing. Tom and B'Elanna will have one child to worry about, but I have a ship full of crew to think of.

"What if I have to order Tom or B'Elanna to put their life at risk? A captain has to be ready to do that. I don't know how the Galaxy-class captains handled it. Can I put the best officer to a dangerous task? Or will I unconsciously pick and choose among those who *haven't* married or had babies? That's not fair to the other crewmen, if certain people can opt themselves out of the risk factor—"

"You're overthinking." Chakotay leaned back a little.

She folded her arms, lowered her chin, and stated, "I'm not. I hope Tom, or B'Elanna, or the other parents to come, if and when, and their children can forgive me—or you—when we have to put one, or both, or all of them . . . on the line."

"Cargo bay."

His watch ended before he noticed. The captain came to take over before Chakotay was really ready to leave the bridge.

Something about their conversation troubled him and made him want to stay up there.

The turbolift hummed around him, content in its purpose to deliver him to the bay as ordered. At least it knew where it was going.

But with Janeway there and no emergency, he made himself let go. For countless men through the history of Earth and of other planets, life on ships was an accepted way. But she was right—it was no kind of family life. Usually it made for long periods away from kith and kin, but months, not years upon years. Even the longest whaling voyages of Earth, hundreds of years ago, were two-year missions, and the crew on board all understood what they were in for.

He had to admit Kathryn was right to worry. They could pretend these things weren't factors, but only pretend.

What else? Stop their shipmates from forming relationships and starting their lives until they were back in Federation space? *Voyager* was an island unto herself, a little community living inside a floating fortress.

He was glad he hadn't made the mistake of telling the captain where he was going for lunch.

The cargo bay, oddly, was one of few places aboard a ship where there was lots of space but no people. Alway immaculate, because the faintest filth could clog up a shuttle's systems and cause big trouble on the go, the bay smelled of cleaning fluids and other control elements—and lunch meat?

The lights were dimmed, and a skyport had been opened to show the stars—as if *Voyager*'s crew hadn't seen enough of stars for a couple of lifetimes. In the middle of the bay's launch roundhouse tarmac was Seven of Nine, quaintly crouched as she spread out a checkered blanket.

Seven was a gorgeous woman standing or sitting, no doubt

about that, and the one-piece molded suit that creased every crease and followed every curve simply added to her mystique, but squatting on the tarmac and using those long arms and spindlelike fingers to spread something as mundane as a picnic blanket absolutely shattered any hope of propriety. Chakotay paused at the entryway for a few seconds, appreciating nature's talent for sculpture.

After a moment, he forced himself to stride in. If she saw him watching her, she wouldn't understand. Deprived of a normal human childhood and adolescence, Seven had never been at ease with the way men looked at her. Having no barometer of social tenderizing with which to judge things as fleeting as physical presence, she didn't know she was an eagle's cry from average.

"What's all this?" he asked.

Seven glanced up at him, then began unpacking a plastic container full of food. "A picnic. My research indicated it was an appropriate third date."

"You didn't have to go to this much trouble . . ."

"If this makes you uncomfortable, I could prepare a less elaborate meal."

"No—don't change a thing. This is *perfection.*"

He sat down on the blanket and crossed his legs. The reduced lighting caused glossy bands on Seven's tightly rolled blond hair. Her large eyes were like cactus flowers on a dune, somewhat severe in their mystery, banded by the few remaining Borg implants on her smooth skin.

Perhaps some people would think it odd that Chakotay had crossed the line and attempted the dreaded 'r' word with her . . . a relationship. More than a friendship, more than crewmates, a step beyond the wisdom of equality the captain had just been talking about, a bond of affection between two people on

Voyager was a species unto itself. This was a closed society. Most of the prospects for romance that the crew would ever encounter were already here. Certain crew members' courting others wasn't unheard of—just rarely successful.

If pressed, Chakotay might've been made to admit that he saw something in Seven, despite her flat-toned voice and her mechanical approach to daily life, leftovers from existence as an assimilated Borg drone. She wasn't the only drone who had been liberated from the Collective, but somehow he sensed she had never been fully assimilated. Somehow her human spirit had survived in a chilling environment and she had remained connected, by however thin a thread, to her individuality. He sensed she didn't perceive her own inner strength, that the captured human child had been pervading enough to cling to herself somewhere deep inside her invaded mind, and she had been assimilated for a very long time. Chakotay doubted he could've hung on so long.

Actually, the picnic *was* perfection. She had "researched" exactly what was supposed to be in the typical, traditional, prescribed picnic. There was even soda pop in replicated bottles and meat that had been rolled out into sandwich-sized squares, and some suspiciously papery potato chips.

"Where did you get all this food? Chell's running the mess hall with an iron hand, if a tongue in cheek. I don't think he'll be as much of a social lubricant as Neelix was."

"Neelix spoke with him over the long-range subspace. He likes the idea of playing 'matchmaker.' "

Chakotay watched her eyes. "You don't know what that means, do you?"

"Yes," she said, and left it at that.

"Have you spoken to Neelix?"

"We have a standing appointment every third day to play kadis-kot by remote, at least until *Voyager* is out of range."

Chakotay tipped his head sadly. "As difficult as that day will be, we all hope it'll come soon. Sometimes I don't think we know what we really want. If it weren't for the captain's ability to cling to one vision and a sense of purpose, I think we would've all scattered long ago, gone off in sixty different directions, searching for some kind of fulfillment . . . or just not survived. Instead we have picnics, games, food . . . and babies for shipmates. Not all bad."

She tried to understand, but he could tell most of his idle chat was floating past her without taking a grip. Seven knew only two kinds of life—the Borg Collective, and the starship.

"You're very pretty in this light," he mentioned.

"Thank you," she said, handing him a plastic plate. "You're very pretty too."

"Oh . . . thanks. My mother used to tell me the same thing."

"I didn't realize." Seven finished laying out the food in a very specific pattern of right angles, and sat down beside him, her spine rod-straight.

"Realize what?" he asked.

"The similarity I bear with your mother. I shall take it as a compliment. Most people regard their mothers with a positive attitude."

"Depends on the mother," he said, "but I liked mine." He picked up one of the bottles of pop and hoped there was something inside other than colored water. "You don't really remind me of my mother. You just made me think of her for a second."

She looked up. "What's the difference?"

He slugged the drink. Cold, but no carbonation. Half right. "I don't know . . . you're not like her in very many ways—hardly any, actually. But she was curious about the things around her.

You both have curiosity in common. And she was a strong person. You have that too."

Seven raised her hand and flexed it.

Chakotay smiled. "Not that kind of strong."

"What other kind is there? Odor?"

This time he rocked back and laughed. "Y'know, you're a lot funnier than anybody gives you credit for."

Perplexed, she watched him laugh. "I did not mean to make a joke."

He nodded and leaned back on his elbow. "Seven, that's the best kind. Hand me a sandwich."

Commander Tuvok sat at the *kal-toh* table in the mess hall, opposite Icheb. He was becoming accustomed to having liberated Borg on the ship, sooner than he had previously calculated. It was Icheb's move.

The glittering pile of tiny rods on the table, each precariously positioned into a geodesic, testified to nearly an hour of gaming. Though the formation appeared chaotic, it could not be so and still maintain its dimensionality. Putting his complex Vulcan faculties to work on the formation, Tuvok calculated the stress points and engineered a multidimensional replica of the geodesic in his mind, then established every possible future arrangement with added rods.

Icheb seemed unable to calculate any possibilities at all. He hovered, a rod in hand, and began to make his move.

A spontaneous cough from the side interrupted Icheb's attempt. A few steps away, Mr. Kim was making a pretense of disinterest. Thus affected, Icheb changed his strategy, moving the rod to a new position.

Tuvok cast a disapproving glance at Kim before addressing

Icheb directly. "In the interest of fair play, I should inform you that Mr. Kim has never defeated me at *kal-toh*."

Icheb paused, considering the new information, processed it, and altered his strategy once again. He moved his rod back to the original position and inserted it into the structure.

Kim sighed. "You should've listened to me."

Icheb said nothing, but clearly doubted himself. Curious that a former Borg, so deeply intertwined in an orderly structure, would be easily confused. Of course, a typical drone had a limited program for purpose and was not encouraged to act independently in any way. Even a simple game was, for Icheb, an insurmountable challenge of mind and design.

On the sideline, Harry Kim's foot accidentally brushed the leg of Tuvok's chair. Tuvok blinked out of his thoughts, analyzed the altered structure, made a conclusion, and inserted his own rod into a position near the top of the geo-design. The structure began to shimmer, and changed its own shape to adjust to his installation.

"Kal-toh is as much a game of patience as it is of logic. An experienced player will sometimes take several hours to decide his next move. In some cases, even days are necessary to properly assess—"

Without taking this as a suggestion, Icheb simply pushed another rod into the structure. Almost immediately!

The structure shimmered again, but this time with vigor, and crackled into a perfect symmetrical shape.

"Kal-toh!" Icheb cried in victory.

Kim actually left the deck briefly. "You beat him!"

Impossible!

Tuvok controlled his reaction in a way he hoped would be admirable to his forebears. Still, the shock penetrated his chest and caused him to skip a breath.

"Congratulations," he said, perforce.

Icheb fidgeted as if he had done something wrong. "I'm sure it was just beginner's luck, sir. I'd offer you a rematch, but I'm due in astrometrics—"

"Another time, perhaps."

Apparently eager for escape, Icheb exited with dispatch. Kim, however, quickly slid into the seat opposite Tuvok.

"He may have to go," Kim said, "but I'm free. And I'm feeling lucky!" He rubbed his hands together and contemplated the sparkling structure between them.

Tuvok forced himself to inhale, then to breathe normally. The structure between them was the manifestation of random chance. It must be. There was no other—

Deceit. Self-deceit.

He stood quickly. "Excuse me, Ensign."

As he stepped abruptly for the door, Kim called, "It's only a game, Tuvok . . ."

He went straight to the sickbay. His arms and legs seemed stiff, his joints aching. Tension could produce those repercussions.

"Tuvok?" The Doctor met him near the door as if expecting him. "Self-diagnosing again?"

"Doctor, you must examine me earlier than scheduled."

"I really don't think there's a reason to—"

"I lost a round of *kal-toh*. To Icheb."

"Oh . . . please make yourself comfortable. I'll see to you immediately. Icheb's an exceptionally bright young man. Did it occur to you that he might simply be a better player?"

The Doctor collected his medical tricorder from its recharge base and began to scan Tuvok even before he was completely settled.

"My loss was the result of another lapse in concentration," Tuvok told him.

The tricorder murmured at his ear. Indeed it seemed several decibels louder than usual. He concluded that he was more sensitive than usual. The device could not be adjusted for volume. Thus it was he, himself, who was malfunctioning.

"I *am* detecting lower neuropeptide levels," the Doctor ultimately admitted.

Tuvok did not meet the searching eyes of the hologram. "As I suspected. My condition's deteriorating."

"It's a minor change," the Doctor said. "We knew it would happen. I simply need to increase your medication."

The Doctor was prone to understate critical problems. Tuvok knew that, yet also appreciated the attempt to comfort him in his concerns. There was no denied fact. The Doctor had no way to treat a Vulcan neurological defect on a long-term basis. *Voyager*'s medical files were up to the highest Federation standard, but that standard had stopped advancing seven years ago. There were no new data to enhance the system, no flow of brilliance from many quarters. Except for information gathered about alien life here in the Delta Quadrant, *Voyager*'s medical facility was in a kind of stasis. When it came to Vulcans, Tuvok himself was the only case study. Thus, the Doctor might log the progress of this disease for use on other Vulcans at a future time, but Tuvok knew his own prospects for improvement.

At which point would he become useless to the ship? Would he sense the changes accurately? Would he be able to be of use to the captain long enough to make a difference for the crew's future?

Should he begin to train someone else in his duties? Simply by virtue of his being a Vulcan, three crewmen would be required to replace him.

He had never wanted to be a teacher . . .

A hypospray pressed to his arm and shook him from his troubled thoughts.

"Thank you, Doctor," he said. Soon his mind would clear.

He stood up, steadied himself, and moved toward the door.

"Commander—"

Tuvok paused, and turned at the Doctor's summons.

The Doctor's expression was solicitous. "I understand your desire for privacy, but maybe it's time we informed the captain."

"*I* will inform her," Tuvok said with unnecessary force, "if and when the disorder begins to affect the performance of my duties."

He managed to exit before the experience began to show upon his face or in his stride.

Was fear an emotion?

CHAPTER 9

"YOUR MOVE."

"Green, grid twelve-ten."

The astrometrics lab was working on automatic, scanning the skies. Seven of Nine listened to the readouts as they murmured in the background, but gave them no undue attention. The machines were at their finest tuning possible and would alert her if there were some disturbance in the scans.

She concentrated instead upon the kadis-kot board on top of her console. On the domescreen optical, a large picture of Neelix's face added a sense of community to the otherwise antiseptic lab. Community was important.

"Red," Seven said, "grid three-thirteen."

She moved her chip accordingly.

"Tricky," Neelix said.

Was this approval of her move? She believed so.

"How is Brax?" she asked as she waited for him to consider his response tactic.

"Wonderful," Neelix said with enthusiasm. "Thanks for asking. I know I can never replace his father, but . . ."

His voice trailed off.

Seven offered encouragement. "I have no doubt the boy looks up to you."

Neelix smiled in a way that gratified her. "Yellow, grid one-one." As she moved his chip in representation of him, he added, "I haven't told anyone, but I'm thinking of asking Dexa to marry me."

"She'd be wise to accept," Seven said. She had found Neelix to be a forthright person, friendly and accepting. Such a marriage would be a prized union.

Neelix was smiling at her. "Enough about my love life. How's yours?"

Something about the question made her aware of herself. This self-awareness was one of the more interesting and disturbing elements of her life without the Collective, yet somehow she was always excited by it.

"I don't have a 'love life,' " she said.

"Oh? What would you call your relationship with Commander Chakotay?"

"It's your turn."

Why did she wish so much for privacy on this subject? She had never cared before what was said between herself and the commander, or who overheard them. Neelix had been kind to her, and encouraging in this new venture, this concept of romance and the joining of two people in a special bond. Perhaps he was succeeding, for this kind of mutuality was traditionally personal. Did she have "a relationship"?

"Actually," Neelix said, "it's yours. At least tell me how he liked the picnic."

She glanced at the domescreen and allowed herself to confide in him. "It was an enjoyable experience for both of us. Thank you for suggesting it."

"Any time." He began another question, but was interrupted by a unit alarm.

Seven dismissed herself from the game board and attended the wailing console.

"What is it?" Neelix asked. His tone of voice suggested that he wished to be back aboard *Voyager,* participating in whatever was about to occur.

"Long-range sensors are detecting extremely high neutrino emissions," she read off the monitor, "accompanied by intermittent graviton flux . . . approximately three light-years away."

Very close. Why had such readings been silent until the ship was so near?

"A wormhole?" Neelix asked.

"I'm not sure. I'll need to run additional scans."

"We can finish our game tomorrow."

Lost in her work, Seven nodded without meeting his gaze. "I'll contact you at the usual time."

She affixed her eyes firmly on the strange readings and forced the equipment to focus, then focus again on the impulses flying into the sensors. The readings were cluttered, indecipherable. Wormhole . . . the data seemed correct, but skittish. It kept changing position.

Seven changed the focus of the sensors several times on a nebula that the starship was quickly approaching—less than one light-year now.

Suddenly the calibrations snapped to clarity. When they did, Seven's human heart began to pound.

*   *   *

Voyager's bridge was the town square of their universe. When critical information arrived, it came here first. Captain Janeway, Chakotay, Tom Paris, and Tuvok had mustered to hear a stunning report from Seven and Harry Kim, and to look at the graphic of the huge churning golden nebula they now skirted. The nebula was heavily clouded, with distinct edges, probably held by magnetic forces that might someday draw all this matter into a single spatial body.

The main screen showed only the stirring sight of the nebular gases. However, an auxiliary monitor brightened with additional information, an analytical graphic of the nebula.

Kathryn Janeway peered at the graphic and fought her churning stomach. The sight wasn't making her ill—it was making her excited. The core of the nebula, like the eye of a hurricane, was clear of gases or matter. Inside that clearing were hundreds of blinking dots.

Seven of Nine stood near the monitor, reporting what she knew so far.

"The emissions are occurring at the center of the nebula," she said. "There appear to be hundreds of distinct sources."

Harry was nearly bouncing on his toes. "Which could translate into hundreds of wormholes!"

Though everyone fidgeted with the thrill of this discovery, Seven remained anchored to the data. "The radiation is interfering with our sensors, but if Ensign Kim's enthusiasm turns out to be justified, it could be the most concentrated occurrence of wormholes ever recorded."

"Any idea where they lead?" Janeway's question gave voice to the frustrated eagerness she felt churning around her from every member of the bridge crew.

"Not yet," Kim said, "but if any *one* of them goes to the Alpha Quadrant—!"

Choked by his own surge of anticipation, he couldn't even finish the sentence.

Tom Paris smiled at him. "Who knows, Harry? Maybe it'll take us right into your parents' living room."

Janeway glanced around at her crew. They were holding their breath—or pretending not to—and waiting for their captain to pick the right wormhole in the next five minutes and drive through it to the rousing cheers of their families at home.

Home . . .

But Janeway wasn't a tour director. It was her job to nurture their hopes while also guarding their very lives. She turned to the main screen and gazed at the enormous lightning-racked tumor in space with puffs of energized matter boiling in great thunderheads the size of entire planets.

"Alter course, Mr. Paris," she began, measuring her volume and degree of enthusiasm. "Ensign Kim, when you speak to your mother, tell her we may need her to move the sofa. All of you, take your duty stations. Seven, tune astrotelemetrics to prioritize those neutrino fluxes."

"Yes, Captain."

Janeway looked around and noted with satisfaction the sudden activity her orders had caused. They still behaved like a ship's crew when it counted. Chakotay was looking one by one at each monitor as he stood near Janeway. Tuvok and Kim went to their stations on the bridge. Seven had quickly gone to the lift and disappeared, heading for astrometrics.

"Mr. Chakotay, let's have red alert. Call all hands."

"All hands, Captain." He pressed the comm on his link panel. "All hands on deck. Red alert. All hands to emergency stations. Report readiness to the first officer."

"Secure for turbulence," Janeway added. "Batten all systems.

Secure deflector shields and man all primary and auxiliary stations shipwide. Clear the outer areas and flush the nonessential plasma systems."

"All departments complying," Chakotay confirmed, monitoring the changes on his private readouts, with each segment of the ship flashing from red to green as the crew mustered from their quarters or the mess hall and systems were manned and locked down. "Uh-oh . . . B'Elanna requests permission to report to engineering."

Janeway glanced at him. "Denied. She's to report to sickbay."

"And you want *me* to tell her?"

"I'll tell her, if you're not up to the challenge."

"Something tells me we'd rather have you alive. Maybe I'll have the Doctor tell her."

"Good idea."

She fell to an uneasy silence. She had to keep her mouth shut now. Sometimes the captain's job was to let everyone else do theirs. They needed time to get settled, countercheck and secure all ship's systems, make sure the shields were stable and the ship was battened down for the storm of storms. Luckily, unlike in a battle situation, she had the time to give.

While she waited, she communed with the nebula. Nebulas were one of the most unpredictable of natural phenomena. They had no patterns of action, and almost no similarities that could be counted upon. Each one was unique, and even once you were inside the currents couldn't necessarily be plotted, considering thousands of individual storms working upon each other at conflicting pressure levels. They were in for a ride.

"Captain, we're secure for turbulence," Chakotay reported, sounding eminently pleased with how well they were doing despite their lack of a chief engineer.

As Paris turned the starship toward the murky mass, the overwhelming size of the nebula began to make itself known. It was greater than any sea. They could barely read the width of it, never mind the height from their vantage point about a third of the way down the body of the obstruction.

"Maybe Chell should add Nebula Soup to his menu," Paris commented when the first shocks of electrical disruption washed across the primary hull and pressed the nacelles downward.

The second jolt was harder. Janeway grabbed the rail. "Shields?"

"Holding," Tuvok responded.

"Bridge to astrometrics."

"Astrometrics. Seven."

"Any more data on those neutrino emissions?"

"Negative, Captain. I still can't get a clear scan."

"Distance to the center?"

"Six million kilometers."

The ship no longer jolted, but now began to shake with a bone-deep vibration that didn't stop. Rather it increased with every kilometer.

"What is it?" she asked.

Tuvok answered, "I'm detecting a tritanium signature, bearing three-four-two mark five."

"Whatever it is," Paris added, "it's close."

Tritanium . . . certainly wasn't anything naturally created in this maelstrom that now kicked them from side to side.

"Evasive maneuvers," she ordered by way of precaution. This wasn't the time or place for a collision.

Paris already had a pattern plotted and slid the ship into a new angle of entry. The vibration began to subside.

"Was it a ship?" Chakotay asked.

"Possibly." Tuvok kept working.

Janeway's instincts wouldn't turn down the alarms in her

head. The ship seemed to be moving smoothly, but tritanium . . . *why* would there be tritanium?

The main screen was a fuming yellow-green cauldron now,
red-veined and flashing, with no points of reference, no way to
judge visually the distance between clumps of active gas and the
poisoned expanses pressing them apart. Even the experienced
eye could make no dependable judgments. Everything would be
a guess—instinct.

"Another tritanium signature!" Kim shouted. "Right on top
of us!"

The captain parted her lips to give an order, to change the
angle of entry again in favor of their strongest shields, when the
ship suddenly boomed again with vibration, ten times worse!

On the main screen, the murk parted and with stunning clarity
a gargantuan Borg cube cut through the mustardy cloud, on a
dead-ahead collision course with *Voyager!*

CHAPTER 10

"Tom!"

Janeway never even had the chance to choose a direction for evasive actions. She blurted the single cry to Paris, lost in the roar of engines and vibration, but the ship was already moving. A good helmsman wouldn't hit something just because he didn't have an order not to.

The ship veered sharply down and to starboard, missing the icebreaker prow of one of the cube's corners. A Borg cube! What were they doing here? Why hadn't the ship's systems recognized the—

When the pressure in her head changed, she shouted, "Get us out of here!"

But Paris had anticipated the obvious and was already turning the starship in a stomach-bending loop downward and under the cube, around and toward the outside of the nebula. Within the first second the nebula gases swarmed in to cut the two vessels off from each other.

On the sensor graphics, the Borg cube's trajectory ran in

nearly a straight line, a completely different angle from the vec-tor *Voyager* had just taken.

"Full impulse!"

Paris's voice was hoarse. "Impulse two-thirds . . . full impulse."

Every heart pounded. Their thud racked Janeway's mind. She gritted her teeth and felt her cold hands on the rail. Five sec-onds . . . ten . . . the nebula parted and belched them out.

"Aft viewers," Chakotay anticipated, and brought up several angles of the nebula as they ran away from it.

"Tom, vector one-eight."

"One-eight . . ."

The ship turned upward and to port. He knew what she was after—to completely change course again in a random direction so their trail would be harder to trace. Every ship had emissions, and those might prove a problem. She might have to shut the im-pulse drive down and let the ship drift to create a cold trail. Also dangerous . . . momentum could be hard to build, and she might need it.

"Are they in pursuit?" she asked, breathless. "Did they see us?"

For several seconds, no one answered. If there were any hints on any dynoscanner, it could pop up almost anywhere. For such big beasts, the Borg cubes could be shockingly stealthy.

Tuvok was the first to dare a conclusion. "There's no evidence that the cube detected us."

No evidence. That meant nothing at all. Just because no evi-dence was found didn't mean there weren't reams of it tucked under covers.

"Where is it now?" Chakotay asked.

Janeway touched the nearest comm. "Astrotelemetrics, have you got a location on the Borg cube? Seven?"

"Yes, Captain, I triangulated on it as it passed. It's now almost three light-years away."

"How could they have not seen us?" Paris asked. "We came within ten meters of their hull!"

"The Borg wouldn't knowingly risk a collision," Tuvok told him. "The radiation must have interfered with their sensors as well as ours."

Harry Kim turned to Janeway. "If they can't detect us, we should go back!"

"I wouldn't recommend that," Seven said from belowdecks. *"My analysis of the tritanium signatures suggests there were at least forty-seven Borg vessels in the nebula."*

"We can't just give up on those wormholes!"

"Oh, yes, we can," Janeway inflicted before this went too far in the wrong direction.

"What if we tried to modify the—"

She raised a hand. "Sorry, Mr. Kim. You may be the captain someday. But not today."

They didn't know what she meant. She felt the scouring gaze of every crewman. They wanted to go home, and they wanted to run away. The fear of Borg assimilation had become very real and immediate for *Voyager*'s crew. Visceral reactions told them to run for their lives.

But run where?

Then, there was the other side of the coin. A herd of angry bulls lay between them and a chance to get home before they were all too old to care. They wanted to go in and take their chances.

Why couldn't they just have a stroke of luck without the baggage?

Forty-seven Borg cubes . . . forty-seven . . .

* * *

87

"How're you feeling?" Tom Paris escorted his unhappy wife from sickbay toward their quarters before boing back on duty.

"I feel put upon, strangled, and insulted."

"Come on! Who insulted you, B'Elanna? You haven't talked to anybody but me and the Doctor—"

"The captain," she grumbled. "Confining me to sickbay during red alert. Me! Sickbay! I'm the chief engineer!"

"Not this week, you're not."

"Why isn't this baby born? What takes so long? She's ready, I'm ready—we should just use the transporter."

Rather than argue with her, he cleared the door of their quarters so she could waddle right inside without pausing. She hated to pause. The momentum was hard to get going again.

She went straight to the only chair in which she was comfortable these days. He provided leverage, and soon she was seated, looking like a pressure cooker about to explode.

He smiled, but ruefully. There wasn't exactly joy in his anticipation, though he found some amusement in her. He flopped down on the edge of the bed and stared at their four feet generally mixed up down there.

"Forty-seven Borg cubes, B'Elanna . . . what were they all doing there? Did we stumble on Borg central? The terrible part is that I don't really care. I don't want to go back there, no matter what we find out. The whole episode scared me down to my socks."

"It's not like you to be afraid," she said.

With a shrug he admitted, "I'm not usually so shaky. I don't know, I've never felt this kind of scared . . . not like I felt when I saw that cube ten feet off the bow. Poor Harry . . . you should've seen his face. He wants to do more than just communicate with his parents over the Pathfinder. He really wants to be back there. Me, I've got nothing to go back for, but usually I can make myself forget. When I looked into Harry's eyes when we turned away from the nebula . . . B'Elanna, all I saw was the reflection of my drive to get out of there and never go back in. What does that make me? A coward?"

"You're not afraid for yourself," she reasoned. "I know you better."

"But I am! I've got a responsibility to stay alive now like never before. I can't take the kind of risks I used to take because now an innocent life is depending on me. I've got no business sticking my neck out anymore. Those are *Borg* out there, not Klingons!"

She gave him a quizzical glare and silently scolded him until he realized what he'd said.

Paris pressed a hand to his face. "I—didn't—mean that the way it sounded."

B'Elanna slouched a little deeper into the chair. "Let me get Seven up here and you can critique us both."

"Don't even joke about it," he moaned. "If we'd been collectivized . . ." He lowered his voice and forced out the rest. ". . . what would've happened to our daughter?"

His wife's harsh expression mellowed at the idea and a brief silence fell between them. Neither of them could voice the true prospects. Would their child have simply been "removed"? Killed as a sort of useless parasite? Or assimilated with no chance for life other than as another Borg drone?

His head spun with terrible waking dreams. "We pretend that all the risk and danger and the not knowing whether we're going to be alive next month isn't here because there's nothing we can do about it. Why worry about something we just have to handle? But we became so casual about it that we're having a baby! What kind of world am I bringing a child into? What business do we have doing this?"

"Little late," she muttered. "But if you don't live life all the way while you have the chance, you're already dead. What's the use of surviving?"

He grumbled a halfhearted agreement and slipped back on an elbow. "This is *tough*. I feel like sending a long-range to my father and apologizing for what it was like to raise me! Do you have any idea what kind of kid I was?"

"Would you rather have died seven years ago," she asked, "so you didn't have to go through what we've all gone through together?"

Surprised by the strange question, he paused to decipher what she meant. "Well . . . no . . ."

"Don't you think our daughter will feel the same way someday? If you asked her if she'd rather be alive on a starship, in trouble now and then, or never be born, what do you think she'd say?"

"Would she say, 'I want to be infiltrated with mechanics and turned into a living robot'?" He shook his head and tried to free himself of the recurring image of that Borg monstrosity rushing toward him and his arms aching as he wrenched the ship away from the very near miss. "When I saw that cube, I suddenly realized that my life really is different now."

Exhausted and lacking a night's sleep in days, B'Elanna suspended her physical frustration and brought out a touch of the circumspection she would need to juggle the coming event with her shipboard responsibilities and the fact that she too had a new set of priorities to work out. She shifted her unbalanced body a little to the left and placed her hand over his until he found the courage to look her in the eyes.

"Welcome to fatherhood," she said.

* * *

The frustrating evening led into an even more frustrating next day. By now everyone knew the captain hadn't made an adventurer's decision.

The crew's reaction ran about fifty-fifty, and tended to change by the hour. At first, the proximity to Borg cubes—so many, many Borg cubes—had pretty much chilled any daring spirits, with the exception of Harry Kim's. As the hours passed, some people grew more hungry for a chance, however speculative, to get home.

Tom Paris, whose hands shook for a good hour after the nebula encounter, had no trouble fixing the ship on a course away from the nebula. A nest of Borg cubes was plenty to crush him back into place.

So when Harry chased him down in the corridor on the way to the bridge, he had an idea what it was about.

"Tom!"

Paris had almost made it to the turbolift. He thought about hurrying, maybe pretending he had wax in his ears. His boots thumped on the corridor deck and guilted him into slowing down so Harry could catch up.

Harry's innocent face appeared beside him. "What are you doing when your watch ends?"

"No plans," Paris said. After all, he couldn't exactly make any plans, considering his family situation. "Why?"

"I've been thinking . . . you and I should have some fun. One last adventure before you get too busy being a father."

Although Paris knew perfectly well what Harry was hedging toward, he tried to redirect. "Did you reserve some holodeck time?"

"I've got a better idea."

They stopped walking as Harry handed him a padd.

Paris almost didn't want to look at it. Unfortunately it was already in his hands and only one glance was needed to confirm the trouble he was very near getting into.

"This is your idea of fun?" he challenged.

"It'll work!" Harry insisted. "We just need to make a few modifications to the flyer—"

"We might as well just hand it over to the Borg!"

"How could that happen with the best pilot in the quadrant at the helm?"

Paris handed the padd back, rather roughly. "Nice try."

He started to walk away.

Harry gripped him by the arm. "If we go to the captain together, she'll be much more likely to approve my plan!"

"I don't want her to approve it."

"Where's your sense of adventure?"

Empathizing with his friend's deeper hopes, Paris freed his arm from the hard sell. To reject Harry this way, and to have to be harsh—it chafed.

"I left my sense of adventure in the nebula," he said sadly. "And I'm not going back for it."

Again he tried to step away.

Desperately, Harry called, "Don't you want to find your way home?"

"I *am* home, Harry."

Instantly, Paris regretted snapping at him. Just the tension . . . all kinds.

Luckily, Harry's reaction of hurt didn't mar his attempt to lighten the moment with one last bit of bait as Paris stepped into the turbolift.

"Captain Proton would never walk away from a mission like this," he suggested.

Paris tried a smile, but it didn't convince either of them that his mood had improved or his fears mellowed.

"Captain Proton doesn't have a wife . . . and a baby on the way."

When the turbolift closed between them, they had more problems than they'd had when they met a few moments ago.

Chakotay sensed the change around the ship. Everyone was quieter, more introspective, dealing with the fact that they had run rather than taken on the complex challenge of finding a wormhole in a Borg haystack. Strange, though—nobody disagreed with the captain's decision to move on. There had been a time, however, when this ship's mission had not been so much precaution and forbearance.

Things had changed. There was a difference from their early days. The crew had flexed, changed, won and lost, released some crewmates, accepted others, and not all of them had signed up for a battleship. Kathryn was right—there were babies now, children, families. Even the crewmen who had intended to spend their lives in uniform had never imagined a single one-way mission where very little could be predicted or planned. They were on this ship, and apparently they were going to be here for a very long time.

Tom and B'Elanna had the right idea. Until now, Chakotay really hadn't been so sure. The change was subtle, but suddenly everyone aboard had concrete confirmation of where their futures were. No wormhole, no magic, no luck, no shortcuts home. If they wanted more than their general duties, they would have to build it for themselves, right here, today.

The astrometrics lab was a quiet place. Usually Seven was here alone, as she was this morning. She seemed surprised to see him when Chakotay entered, and reacted in a charmingly human way. Her eyes were like birds, the rest of her like a hungry dream.

"If you've come for my daily report," she offered, "it's not complete."

Chakotay tried not to swagger. "Actually, I'm here in an unofficial capacity. I was wondering if you'd like to get together again."

"To do what?"

Ah, the old-time loaded question. Did she have any idea of the sheer number of possible answers to that one? He ought to rattle off a few and completely confuse her. She was a lot funnier than she thought.

Or maybe Chakotay's sense of humor was warped. He should have himself tested.

He leaned on the console and shifted a little closer than officers usually prefer. She didn't back away.

"That would depend on your 'research,' " he said. "Would a quiet dinner be an appropriate fourth date?"

Seven's eyes widened. "I believe it would be a more appropriate fifth date."

Now who had the sense of humor?

He smiled and played her game. "I'm willing to skip ahead if you are . . ."

"How far ahead?"

"Well . . . let's do some research."

His finger coiled under her chin, tipping her face toward his. Her eyes were feathered creatures enchanted by the mystery of the moment's sudden silence. Beneath them the console murmured a little music of its own.

His lips never touched hers, though he tasted her breath and felt the warmth of her skin. She drew back at the last moment, just an inch. Despite the hesitation, Chakotay felt she wanted more, just as he did.

She reached up and slipped her hand over his, then drew his

hand away from her face, though she didn't move back or release her grip or its promise.

"Tonight," she said. "We will skip ahead."

VESSEL IDENTIFIED: *U.S.S. VOYAGER*. COLLECTIVE MEMORY
CONFIRMED.
JANEWAY, COMMAND
CHAKOTAY, EXECUTIVE
SEVEN OF NINE, BORG DISENGAGED PRIORITY REESTABLISH.

Analysis accepted.

She enjoyed her body, her muscles. She enjoyed her mind and sense of independent thought. These privileges she kept to herself. She was the only one of her kind. She kept ambition to herself.

Around her the comforting maze of blocky mechanical constructions, shafts, scaffolds, utility cubes, tubes, maturation chambers, alcoves, regeneration units, and the other billions of individual components making up the hive concept, duplicated in every Borg cube everywhere, gave her strength of purpose.

WE WILL PURSUE AND ASSIMILATE. STIMULATE CENTRAL
PLEXUS

"No."

A million voices sounded in her head. Monotone, mechanical, purposeful. She was serene.

"They haven't compromised our security. Let the vessel continue. I'll keep an eye on them."

* * *

COMPLYING. MONITOR *U.S.S. VOYAGER* PROGRESS, JANEWAY COMMANDING

In her enormous and far-reaching mind, she tasted the body of *Voyager* soaring through space. Electrical impulses. Molded metal and fibrous cables. Complex matrices. She smelled the hull shapes.

This was her exclusive breakfast. She was the lone appreciator. Not a drone, not an assimilant, not a fragment. The isolated and spectacular potentate of a billion-celled body, she was the center of the central plexus, the queen.

The Borg Queen.

CHAPTER 11

THE BIOBED FELT COLD AND DID NOT BECOME WARM. SEVEN OF Nine fixed her eyes on the ceiling and steadied herself to her purpose. This would be a weekly maintenance check like none other, for after the next few moments her future would be altered.

"You're fine," the Doctor said, "aside from some minor inflammation around your biradial clamp. Let me know if it starts to bother you."

He put down his tricorder. The examination was complete. Seven was expected now to stand and leave the sickbay.

She continued lying on the biobed, listening to the blips and bubblings of mechanical analysis deep within the systems of the sickbay consoles and processors. A pleasant noise. She recalled the idea of sound as a mode of entertainment from a deeply seated memory which had no roots, but floated free in her mind.

The Doctor almost went back to his work when he realized she had not altered her position.

"Is there something else?" he asked.

Seven hesitated. This move was unwise. It would weaken her. She should cling to her isolation and strength.

Must she give up her strength in order to grow?

She cleared her throat. "Do you remember three months ago, when my cortical node shut down?"

The Doctor struck an expression. "How could I forget?"

"You . . . you said it might be possible . . . to remove the fail-safe device that was causing the problem . . ."

"Has it been giving you trouble again?" He moved closer to her.

"No. But . . . I've . . . reconsidered your offer to extract it."

The Doctor paused. His voice grew softer. "I've been hoping you would."

An uneasy pause broke their conversation as Seven sat up on the biobed and noted that her hands and legs were as cold as the cushion.

"You said it would require several surgeries . . ."

He fought down a smile. "Actually, in anticipation of your change of heart, I've studied the problem in more detail. I now believe I can reconfigure the microcircuitry with a single procedure." He was eager about his new knowledge, proud of himself in his anticipation.

How could he know so conveniently that she might return with such a request? She hadn't thought about such a daring choice until . . . until Chakotay.

"You'll be free," the Doctor went on, "to experience the full range of emotions. Everything from a hearty belly laugh to a good cry."

She looked down at the long plane of her stomach, and wondered why anyone would laugh at it. "How soon can you do it?"

"Today, if you'd like." He obviously preferred a quick turnover, though he didn't outwardly offer any pressure or timelines.

"My watch ends at eighteen hundred hours."

"It's a date!"

His joy disturbed her. She was afraid of alteration. But how could there be progress without change?

Forcing herself to accept what she had now scheduled, she pushed off the bed and started toward the door.

"Speaking of dates," the Doctor called, "once the fail-safe is gone, you'll be free to pursue more intimate relationships."

He bounced on his holo-toes.

Seven looked at him. "I'm aware of that," she proclaimed, attempting to seem in control.

"If you decide you need help with that aspect of your humanity," he said, eyes twinkling, "I'm always at your disposal."

Was this a sexual proposition?

Unlikely.

"I appreciate that," Seven responded.

The Doctor brightened. "Really?"

"Yes," she said, her voice more gravelly than usual. "But I already have all the 'help' I need."

He seemed briefly confused, then realized what she was talking about. "Ah . . . of course. You'll undoubtedly be running more simulations with the Chakotay hologram."

Seven shifted her feet, causing her body to sway in a motion she had found common among her human shipmates, and this time, oddly, she found good use for the "language."

"No, actually," she told him proudly. She almost said more, then in deference to Chakotay's privacy, kept her silence.

Perhaps he inferred her meaning. Perhaps not.

"I'll see you at eighteen hundred hours," she finished, and let him go on guessing.

* * *

2100 hours

Why was someone working the transporter?

Chakotay stood up sharply at the whine of beaming technology squirming through his head when he least expected it—and *where* he least expected. His own quarters?

Instantly he suspected an invasion and made crazy plans in his head to get to the nearest phaser, or at least grab a candle off the table and shove it in the face of some misguided alien offender.

Instead, the form beaming in took on a decidedly attractive shape rather quickly and he realized he was in no danger. So to speak.

"Am I early?"

Seven's low-pitched grainy voice sounded much more sultry and steamy braced up by soft music and candlelight than it usually did when she was making reports to the captain. The candle's glow from the dinner table flickered in her bullion hair and fiddled with the bouquet of flowers she held against her sculpted breasts.

Since when had beaming become such an enchantment?

Chakotay shook the surprise off his face, realizing she didn't understand why he was braced for action. "No—you're right on time. Is there something wrong with the door?"

She moved toward him. "I didn't think it would be discreet to be seen carrying flowers to the first officer's quarters."

He took them from her and studied them lightly. "Thanks. Your 'research'?" When she smiled, he added, "I should put these in wat—"

The flowers hit the deck. Seven had him in a headlock—with her lips. The scent of her filled his head, a clean and aromatic scent of flower petals and shampoo, a touch of perfumed oil and the sharp zap of passion.

Oh, yes . . . there were more important things than flowers, weren't there? What kind of an idiot leaves the side of a gorgeous woman to tend a batch of artificially generated flowers? What was he thinking?

She only broke off so they could each take a breath.

"I've been told," she whispered, "that anticipation of the first kiss is often uncomfortable. I wanted to alleviate the tension."

Chakotay drew her even closer than her strong arms had bonded them. "That was very considerate of you . . . what about the second kiss?"

Her eyes were large enough to reflect the candle and the soft utility lighting behind the ceiling boards to an impossible depth. For a woman whose humanity had been so long lost, she was packed with echoes of life and compassion. Chakotay could look through those windows and see everything—*everything.*

"I'll have to check the database," she roughly murmured.

But he didn't wait. Behind her back his arm tightened. He spread his fingers across her spine until he felt the flare of her hip. A little more pressure, and she sank deeper against him. His lips went to her as fluidly as lilies to sunlight.

For a stiff and soldierly person, Seven melted against him in a way he would never have expected. This should've been much harder for both of them, the way she was, the way he was—the custodians of apartness and untouchability they had fostered in themselves on this ship for the sake of caution suddenly dissolved and were replaced by visceral needs and joys. This was *fun,* plain old happiness—something she had hardly known and that he had almost forgotten.

"Senior officers report to the bridge."

The captain's voice rammed down Chakotay's spine like a needle. What was this—some kind of dime novel? Who had timing this bad!

He thought about ignoring the call, playing sick, dead, assimilated, anything—

"Yellow alert. All hands to stations."

Assimilated . . . oh . . . hell.

Breathless and confounded, he took this radiant and rare young woman by the shoulders and deprived himself of her. Despite the interruption, she had a glint of amusement in her eyes. She liked the spontaneous parts of the game more than she had yesterday.

Chakotay made a sound of dissatisfaction deep in his throat, but he was probably the only one to hear it. Ship's damn business, dammit.

"Next time," he vowed, "we deactivate the comm system."

Chakotay didn't look very happy when he arrived on the bridge with Seven right behind him, but Janeway wasn't interested in why. He seemed to forget his own problems as he glanced around and saw that everyone else was already on station.

Janeway, Tuvok, Kim, and Paris were already at work at their various stations, but all of them were looking at the same bright new trouble that had opened up before the ship without a single blip of warning. The main screen showed a huge view of the impossible—a gigantic energetic hack mark right through space itself.

The colors made Chakotay wince as he hurried to her side. "What is it?"

"Judging from the tachyon emissions," she said, "some sort of temporal rift."

"How's it being generated?" Seven asked from behind Chakotay's shoulder.

Janeway glanced at her, annoyed at being prodded for information she clearly didn't have, or she'd have told them without being asked. "That's what we're trying to figure out," she droned impatiently.

"Could the Borg be doing something?" Harry Kim asked. "I just don't believe they missed us last time."

"They're a long way behind us, Harry," Paris warned, suggesting in a nice way that he shut up about it.

"Not long enough."

"All systems to bear on the rift," Janeway ordered. "Let's have an analysis. Is it light? Energy? A reflection? Why is it giving us temporal disturbance?"

"I hate time-travel," Chakotay grumbled as he punched the controls and tried to focus the sensors. Beside him, Seven was curiously silent. He was closer to her than he needed to be.

"Is it what is appears to be? A cut in space?" Janeway demanded.

"Yes," Seven responded. "It possesses readable dimension and there is physical space within the separations."

Tuvok's steady voice went up a notch. "I'm detecting nadion discharges on the other side of the rift."

"Weapons fire?" Chakotay said.

"It's possible," responded the Vulcan. "The signature appears to be Klingon."

A look of surprise passed from face to face, but there was no time to speculate.

"Red Alert," said Janeway.

An alarm sounded at Tuvok's station. "There's a vessel coming through," he announced.

"Klingon?" Chakotay asked.

"No," Tuvok reported, and turned to look up at the screen. *"Federation."*

Before anyone could respond to the shocking information or inquire whether this were some distorted error erupted to tease them into misery and disappointment. A ploy, a distraction, a red herring—

Janeway put her hand out to stop any jumping to conclusions. They watched, held rapt, as a battered shuttle of some unfamiliar design came rocketing through the temporal slash!

"We're being hailed!" Kim blurted.

"On screen!" Janeway demanded control with her tone.

The viewscreen instantly changed to reveal the smoky interior of a cockpit, and at the controls a woman in her late sixties, wearing a Starfleet field jacket.

Aunt Louise?

The crew was stunned at what they saw, at the faded echo of their captain as if computer-aged in some crime file, but Janeway had seen trickier tricks and wasn't buying it.

"Recalibrate your deflectors to emit an anti-tachyon pulse," the woman ordered. *"You have to seal that rift!"*

Janeway didn't bother to ask what her Aunt Louise was doing in the Delta Quadrant, driving a shuttle with Federation markings, or when she'd become an admiral. Her wariest instincts popped up to protect her from making assumptions.

"It's usually considered polite to introduce yourself before you start giving orders."

"Captain, a Klingon vessel is coming through," Tuvok quickly warned.

"Close the rift!" the older woman shouted.

Defiant, Janeway waited for an explanation, using the threat of Klingon incursion through the rift as leverage.

The admiral was unimpressed. *"In case you didn't notice, I outrank you, Captain. Now do it!"*

A distorted image of a weirdly arranged Klingon ship appeared deep inside the rift.

With controlled urgency Tuvok quickly reported, "More nadion discharges, Captain."

Abruptly, Janeway made a decision. "Recalibrate shields," she ordered.

"Deflectors recalibrated," Tuvok said instantly. He'd been ready.

"Prepare anti-tachyon emission."

"Anti-tachyon emission broadcasting, Captain," Seven responded. "Converting now, triangulated on the rift, port to starboard."

"Ready broadcast system stabilizers and all overload precautions. I'm not ready to burn out at somebody else's say-so."

She made a little inflection on the words *somebody else.*

"Ready," Chakotay said, eagerly taking over that duty.

"Activate."

As the deflector beam blasted steadily from *Voyager*'s dish, Janeway felt her throat close up with tension. Why was there an aged version of herself on that shuttle? She already knew part of the answer. Temporal disruption . . .

Where was she in the future? Captured by Klingons? In the middle of a war that hadn't happened yet? Had she arrived there tomorrow or thirty years from now?

Her heart pounded in her chest. She battled for a steady demeanor. Her crew was watching.

Before them, the rift flashed, burned, and pressed its lips together like some galactic child in defiance after a scolding. No more Klingons. Simple enough.

Now for the complicated part.

She faced off with the ghostly admiral in the damaged shuttlecraft. "I did what you asked . . . now tell me what the hell is going on."

BORG CUBE TRANSMISSION INTERCEPTED
FEDERATION SHUTTLECRAFT, TEMPORAL INCONSISTENCY

DETECT ANTI-TACHYON EMISSION OVERLAPPING TEMPORAL
WAVES

"Let me see them on my screen."

The Borg Queen inhaled deeply the coming stimulation. She flexed her shoulders and spread her fingers, felt her ribs and thighs tighten within the skintight insulation suit with its molded pieces pressing her like a million fingertips.

Their science had tapped into a transmission. The floating viewscreen swept down from above and came to her eye level, showing a vision of a woman with familiar eyes. The woman's hair was silvered, her cheekbones sharp, her lips thin. Her pointed chin was fitted over a gaunt neck, and below that an unfmiliar uniform with Starfleet markings.

"Identify," the Queen summoned.

SUBJECT IDENTIFICATION JANEWAY, KATHRYN ADMIRAL,
STARFLEET

"What is the admiral's current age?"

ENDGAME

AGE: SIXTY-EIGHT POINT FIVE-TWO FEDERATION STANDARD
YEARS

"Audio feed."

On the screen, the vision of Admiral Janeway spoke words of great interest, great substance.

"I've come to bring *Voyager* home."

CHAPTER 12

"WELCOME ABOARD."

Kathryn Janeway gazed up from the forgiving cushion of her senior officers as a figure finished materializing on the transporter platform.

The individual whose identity was so mysteriously apparent also gazed around, but not at the people, not at Chakotay and Tuvok or at Janeway herself. *Admiral* Janeway instead gazed around at the interior of the ship itself. That something as mundane as a tranporter room could carry such obvious nostalgic gravity made the situation particularly surreal.

Then, as if walking into her own back garden, she stepped down from the platform. She moved finally to Chakotay and Tuvok, now standing a little apart from Janeway.

"Tuvok," she murmured. "Chakotay . . . it's good to see you."

Uh-oh. Janeway watched the admiral's expression—and she recognized that tone. What the hell was that tone doing here?

The admiral's voice sounded strange, though, like Janeway herself speaking through a paper funnel. Normal enough—

mostly we hear our own voices through the echo chamber of our skulls. Give or take the odd log review, she wasn't used to listening to herself.

Herself . . .

She flinched when the admiral suddenly turned to her. "I'm sure you have questions."

"Only a few," Janeway drawled.

"Then I suggest we go to my . . . to *your* ready room."

"You know the way."

Well, why not? The obvious had inflicted itself upon them. Time to become explorers.

The admiral led the way. It was one method of confirming that she was the person she appeared to be. They walked the ship in silence, like a tour of a tomb. Janeway met Chakotay's eyes once, only once, but never connected with Tuvok. They all had the same feeling. The instinct to tell when something was really wrong despite the casual walk-and-talk had become a daily diet on *Voyager.*

As they approached the corridor entrance to the ready room, she motioned Chakotay and Tuvok to hold back. Perhaps it was her knowledge of herself speaking—she really wasn't sure yet— but the admiral would speak more freely if she only had her own reflection listening.

Tuvok merely lowered his head in acceptance. Chakotay took hold of her elbow for an instant, then almost immediately let go. The touch was worth its weight in dilithium.

She offered him a passive reassuring glance, nothing except a promise that she would look after herself, and followed the admiral's thin silvery form into the ready room.

The door closed behind her. This was like being in a carnival fun house, except for the fun part.

Admiral Janeway drew a long breath through her nose as if she had stepped into a meadow of wildflowers. "Fresh coffee . . ."

"Would you like a cup?" Janeway asked.

The admiral looked at the steaming thermal carafe on the captain's desk. "No. I gave it up years ago. I only drink tea now."

Annoyance prickled the captain's neck. Since when? Caffeine was caffeine. Was the admiral trying to fit in to some kind of prefab image?

"I told the curator at the museum," the admiral went on, "that if he wanted to make the ready room more authentic, he should always keep a steaming pot of coffee on the desk."

"Voyager's in a museum?"

"Voyager," the admiral said proudly, *"is* a musem. On the grounds of the Presidio." She moved to the wide curved viewport through which multiple stars and one rogue nuclear storm performed brainless. "On a clear morning, you can see Alcatraz from here."

And the irony of that is . . .

Captain Janeway inhaled the moment, held her breath, and pressed down the chittering in her stomach. This was big. Getting bigger.

"You made it back to Earth . . ."

The admiral nodded, but didn't meet her eyes. She moved back to Janeway's desk and picked up the coffee cup. "Unfortunately, our favorite coffee cup didn't get home in one piece. It was chipped during a battle with the Fen Domar."

"Who?" Ah, stupid question time. The value of the senseless blurt.

"You'll run into them in a few years."

Janeway held up a hand before the admiral continued. "You know what? I don't think I should be listening to details about the future."

Instantly her two personalities—the two still inside this body—began wrestling. The Temporal Prime Directive, the risk of the future, complications radiating from the flap of the butterfly's wing all came into raging conflict with her explorer's duty, her command responsibility to tend her crew and to bring this ship home *any way possible*—

What was the right thing to do? Refuse to listen? Or demand to be told?

She wanted to ask everything. Everything! She wanted to hedge her bets, make the challenging decisions, put to use her vaulted experiences collected at such risk and strain here in the Delta Quadrant. She wanted to be an adventurer on purpose instead of by accident!

"The almighty Temporal Prime Directive," the admiral drawled with acrid contempt. "Take my advice. It's less of a headache if you just ignore it."

Janeway's reaction again was mixed. Contempt for regulations? Respect for them was all that had kept *Voyager* held together as a Starfleet ship out where, where there was no Starfleet watching.

"You've obviously decided to ignore it," she said, "or you wouldn't be here."

"A lot's happened to me," the admiral admitted, "since I was you."

The odd pronouncement made Janeway angry. She had a visceral reaction and rubber-banded in the opposite direction from where the admiral wanted to go. Childish? Maybe.

"Well, I'm still me and this is still my ship. So no more talk about what's going to happen until I decide otherwise. Understood?"

"All right," the admiral accepted, too quickly. "Let's talk about the past.

"Three days ago you detected elevated neutrino emissions in a nebula in grid nine-eight-six. You thought it might be a way home. You were right. I've come to tell you to take *Voyager* back to that nebula—"

"It was crawling with Borg!"

"I've brought technology that will get us past them."

Magic from the future. Pretty damned convenient. Doubts raged in the captain's head. Nothing was this easy. Nothing good, anyway.

"I don't blame you for being skeptical," the admiral told her. "But if you can't trust yourself, who can you trust?"

"For the sake of argument," Janeway ventured, "let's say I believe everything you're telling me. This future you come from sounds pretty good. *Voyager*'s home, I'm an admiral, there are ways to defend against the Borg, my ready room even gets preserved for posterity—"

"So why would you want to tamper with such a rosy time line? To answer that, I'd have to tell you more than you want to know."

Janeway glared at the admiral. There was no such thing as *more* than she wanted to know.

The admiral leaned against the edge of the desk, her thigh meeting the desk at a familiar point on the muscle. Janeway found herself staring at the desk and the admiral's leg.

"If you don't do what I'm suggesting," the older woman pressed on, "it's going to take you another sixteen years to get home. And there are going to be casualties along the way."

The revelation was a punch in the gut. It was the voice of failure, of hopelessness and anticlimax. All her effort, her careful thoughts, her wakening nights wondering if she was doing the right thing day to day, minute by minute—to spend their best years rushing at high warp to an unhappy future.

Unhappy? How did she know that? Nothing sounded so bad, nothing the admiral had said or implied . . . why, then, was the admiral here?

Why would I be here? Why would I risk the futures of our crew and billions of others? No tampering with time came without ripples. Why is she here?

Casualties . . . there were always casualties. Even if they had never left on this mission, never been thrown into the Delta Quadrant, even if they stayed in their hometowns there would be accidents. Life would still happen. There were diseases and troubles and random acts that might have taken them from each other. You didn't going around rearranging time to prevent the symphony of life from not exactly going your way. Why not? Because you didn't dare.

I don't dare. Why does she?

"I know exactly what you're thinking," the admiral said, eyeing her with a posture of superiorizing that Janeway suddenly vowed to curb from now on.

"You've also become a telepath?" she grumbled.

The admiral nodded. "I used to be you, remember? You're asking yourself, is she really who she says she is or is this some kind of deception. For all you know, I could be a member of Species Eight Four Seven Two in disguise."

Annoyed, Janeway pressed a smile of irritation out of her lips. The other woman had her over a barrel. If all this was what it appeared to be, she was at a terrific disadvantage. If *she* had become a Starfleet admiral and she was really here talking to a superior officer, then Admiral Janeway had authority over her. If this were any other admiral than herself plucked out of time, what would her obligations be?

But there was undeniable possessiveness born of the past seven unexpected years of trial and isolation. Reflex insisted she should retain complete command here, she must. This had to remain her ship until *Voyager* could be delivered to the Alpha Quadrant.

"Have your people examine my shuttle," the admiral said, reading her mind again. "Tell them to take a close look at the weapons systems and the armor technology. In the meantime, the Doctor can confirm my identity."

Such precautions made sense, but also seemed like colossal wastes of precious time. If Janeway believed her own protests about not wanting to know the future, then the wise thing to do would be to pack this admiral back on her shuttle and stuff her through that rift. Get rid of the temptation. The longer the admiral stayed here, the more the chance for contamination. Keeping her here, examining her, her shuttle—those were risks in and of themselves. The crew would begin to know what was going on. The technicians would log their encounters with whatever was on that shuttle. They would never forget. Tricorders all over the ship would have recorded information. Other than throw such a resource overboard, Janeway couldn't deny the plain fact that she would process and use the information. Any other course of action would be prohibitively cautious. It would be like having a tin of water in a lifeboat. Sooner or later, she would drink.

"We'll call you 'admiral,'" she told the other woman, "and we'll show you all the respect you seem to be due. You know the future and I don't. For all I know, you could be mentally deranged."

"Pretty picture," the admiral shot back.

"We all get old," Janeway had ready. "Sometimes infirmities come. Don't you think I know that?"

The admiral said, "You're pretending to be unaffected by me. I know when you're not being honest. We're the same person—"

"We *used* to be the same person. When you came through that rift, we became two people. You look like me, and we have a common past. We're just like any set of twins now. Our future may not be common at all. Mine is yet to happen and I have to play the game that way."

"The survivors of *Voyager* deserve better than what they got," the admiral said. This time she was angry.

Captain Janeway gestured to the corridor entrance, inviting the admiral to make good on her claims. "We're not survivors yet. We haven't made land."

Seven of Nine sat at the helm of the admiral's shuttle in the starship's bay. Sensations of concern plagued her. What would the captain decide?

Seven was uneasy, though she battled for control. Things were about to change again. In her life, the changes had all been serious, dramatic, sudden and encompassing. Assimilation by the Borg, then life as a drone for many years, ruptured by discovery of her individual self, the little girl so long erased—of late she had not only accepted human individuality but begun to explore it. And now she was seeking the great prize of individuality, the fulfillment lauded in literature and in the eyes of her fellow human beings—a bond of romance and devotion with another human being.

"The armor appears to be autoregenerative," she reported, watching the data scroll before her on the small screens. She worked the controls, changing the graphics to the "armored" stage. "When the system is enabled, specialized nanites reconfigure the molecular structure of the hull to form ablative layers."

The process was not unlike Borg adaptation techniques. Nanites read the surroundings, then changed to accommodate them.

"The armor's just the tip of the iceberg." B'Elanna Torres spoke from the rear of the shuttle's interior, where she crouched with a correlative analysis tricorder on the technology back there. "She's got omnispectral stealth technology and some sort of transphasic photon torpedoes—" Her voice cut off as she struggled out of her crouch, her body betraying both balance and grace. She moved forward to the helm and scanned the pilot's headrest. "And this . . . I'm guessing it's a neural interface. But I couldn't begin to tell you how it works. Of course, there's one thing this vessel isn't equipped for." She squeezed between the seats and added, "A pregnant crewman." Looking down at her primary problem, she knocked and said, "It's time to come out now."

"Ideally," Seven said, "the child won't be born until Thursday at twelve hundred hours."

B'Elanna gawked at her. *"You* joined the baby pool?"

"I'm trying to broaden my participation in crew activities." Seven frosted her expression, keeping to herself the mysterious joy she would feel if she actually won a pointless bet.

B'Elanna struggled to lower herself into the seat. "My life would be so much easier if I'd never met Tom Paris."

Reacting, Seven experienced an inner shock.

"You regret your relationship with him?"

"I was joking," B'Elanna said quickly.

"Then you're happy . . . being part of a couple?"

Despite her obvious discomfort, a passive expression came over B'Elanna's face. Soon, she smiled.

"Yeah," she said. "I am."

* * *

A brain. Human. But not just any brain—*her* brain. Their brain.

Life was simpler in Ireland in the 1800's. Plague, famine, workhouses, overlords—simple little problems. Did somebody say "time travel"?

"My scans of the admiral's cerebral cortex turned up something interesting," the Doctor reported as he stood beside the captain, studing the graphic on the freestanding console in sickbay. He punched a control and the picture changed. It zoomed on one of the brain's lobes, and there focused upon a distinct nonbiological implant.

"What is it?" she asked.

"I'm not sure." The Doctor frowned in both his expression and his voice. "I've never seen this kind of implant before."

Was this evidence? Should she not trust the admiral now? Was the admiral indeed herself at a future time, but being manipulated by some unknown intelligence? A puppet? A trick?

"Alien technology?" Captain Janeway asked.

The Doctor hit a control, and the implant came up in close view on his screen.

"The mircocircuitry has a Starfleet signature."

"Of course it does," Admiral Janeway said. The Doctor and the captain turned to her in surprise. The admiral was now seated, back rod straight, on the biobed.

"Admiral?" The doctor asked.

Admiral Janeway gestured toward the doctor's screen. "You invented it. Twelve years ago, from my perspective."

A self-satisfied smile spread over the doctor's face. "I'm sorry, Admiral," he said, "I didn't realize."

"What, that I was eavesdropping? I may be old but my hearing is excellent, thanks to your exemplary care over the years."

"So," the Doctor hesitated, as if somewhat embarrassed at inquiring into his own future successes, "this implant I'm going to invent—what does it do?"

"It's a synaptic transceiver that allows me to pilot a vessel equipped with a neural interface."

"Fascinating," the doctor said curiously. "Tell me. What other extraordinary breakthroughs am I going to make?"

"Doctor," Janeway scolded softly.

"Sorry, Captain," he acceded. "But you can't blame a hologram for being curious."

"Just finish your report."

"Yes, ma'am. My scans indicate that the two of you are genetically identical. The admiral is you, approximately twenty-six years from now."

The admiral glowed with satisfaction.

So far, nothing new. Just a sniggering confirmation. Janeway would've been happier with a spy or a trick. Confirmation of the admiral's story just tightened the Gordian knot.

She was about to speak again, to order more tests on the implant—as much as they could get without invading the admiral's intimate privacy or imprisoning her—when Seven strode elegantly in with a padd.

The admiral moved toward her, almost reached out, then stopped herself.

"Hello, Seven," she murmured.

Janeway stiffened. The room was suddenly a seance. The admiral seemed to be speaking to a ghost.

The captain's hands turned cold as she held the bitter clue.

Seven stared at the admiral like a confused child. She didn't like the disrupting fact of the admiral's presence chewing up the security of the moment.

Finally she broke from the awkward communion and in a decidedly human defiance turned to her captain. "The technology aboard the admiral's ship is impressive." She handed the padd to Janeway. "Much of it appears to have been designed to defend against the Borg."

The clue turned even more icy. Major encounters with the Borg? Enough that Federation technology concentrated on it, made it a priority?

How much would such knowledge affect decisions from now on, the captain wondered. She commanded a starship commissioned to protect and defend the Federation down to the last life aboard. Did this mean she should turn the ship around and fight until there was nothing left, to fulfill her mission as a Starfleet officer first and forget her role as mother to the immediate nestlings? What was her obligation now?

Might as well get both feet wet.

"Could we install these systems on *Voyager?*" she asked.

So much for divorcing herself from the future.

"The stealth technology is incompatible," Seven reported. "But I believe we can adapt the armor and weapons."

The charged moment fractured her from those around her.

Luckily, the admiral had accepted that the decisions still belonged to Kathryn Janeway the First.

"Well, Captain?"

Janeway eyed her with undisguised annoyance. She didn't like being pressured, but—

The Borg . . .

She turned to Seven. "Do it."

CHAPTER 13

Captain's Personal Log
Stardate 54973.4

We've begun outfitting Voyager *with Admiral Janeway's up-grades. There are dozens of crewmen in environmental suits crawling all over my ship, more than we've had working in space for over a year. Maybe I'm getting soft, but it makes me nervous to have them out there. I've gotten used to the idea that the ship is our cave, our protective shell, and really our entire universe. If they're not aboard, I can't feel as if they're safe.*

Possibly my unease comes from the fact that we're mounting what adds up to alien technology on our only lifeboat. I really don't know this woman. I know who she used to be . . . I know what she appears to be. But the rest is a mystery. The question is—should I let it remain a mystery?

Despite her personal discomfort, Torres is overseeing the conversion. The engineering department is fairly swarming with activity. We've pulled crewmen from almost every other section on the ship, just to have enough hands at work to do this quickly. I have to trust her to notify me if there's anything we might not be able to control. I will not give up control to the admiral, no matter what she claims to be or know. I have to work in the present. That's my only anchor.

All this activity, and it might come to nothing more than a blip on the Borg Queen's victory roster. Compared to the complexity and sheer size and numbers of the Borg Collective in the Delta Quadrant, Voyager *is a very, very tiny force. We have to be careful not to forget.*

How can I know the right thing to do? This ship is a spark in a forest fire when it comes to fighting the Borg. On the other hand, if the admiral's right and we can blast our way through the Borg and into the correct wormhole—something on which I'm still reserving both judgment and hope—I might be morally and dutifully obliged to do just that, to return the ship to the Federation and Voyager's *firepower to the whole of Starfleet.*

If only there were a regulation for this—maybe I'll install one when I make admiral.

As soon as the major modifications are complete, we'll reverse course and head back to the nebula. Though I've certainly had some strange experiences in my career, nothing compares to the sight of my future self briefing my officers on technology that hasn't been invented yet.

But everyone is working hard, and the mood on the ship is one of cautious optimism. If I give them that one gift, at least they will have had a shining new hope for a little while. Janeway out.

"Computer, begin regeneration cycle."

Seven of Nine settled into her alcove, bringing with her troublesome feelings of uncertainty. Regeneration would clear her mind, calm her thumping heart.

The computer murmured its response, reassuring bleeps and twinkling noises which took her back to a more secure time, the immeasurable years as one of the Collective, absorbed in a life without questions.

Seconds passed, only seconds before she was without body or form, drifting. Her biofunctions and cybernetic implants began to merge in their sustaining function.

A green glow formed in her mind. Within it, faces, many faces. The captain . . . the admiral . . . dreams of past and future . . . all just out of reach as she stretched the fingers of her thoughts.

Soon, a voice in the green mist.

"Seven of Nine. Tertiary Adjunct of Unimatrix Zero One."

Seven felt her body tighten. The seductive voice of the Borg Queen.

Her eyes snapped open. There was no more *Voyager.* Only the green glow. Within it hovered the head and chest of the Borg Queen, with just a hint of shoulders.

"It's been too long," the Queen murmured. Her pasty lips curled up at the edges into a bittersweet smile.

Seven tried to look around, but eyes were not necessary to know she was in the Borg Queen's lair.

My feet, my body, are still on Voyager. *I should not be here, in a cube. How has she tapped into my mind?*

"What do you want?" she asked.

The Queen hovered softly, without support. "Do I need a reason to visit a friend?"

"We're not friends."

"No. We're more than that. We're family."

Such insult. Seven's nerve quaked.

* * *

ENDGAME

FAMILY: TWO OR MORE PERSONS RELATED BY GENETIC
CODE. TWO OR MORE PERSONS WITH COMMON BACKGROUND
AND DESIRES. TWO OR MORE PERSONS BOUND BY——

"But while we're on the subject of old friends," the Queen began again, "I see *Voyager* just got a visitor."

How could she know? Did she have tracers planted on *Voyager?*

Am I the tracer?

"She's come from the future," the Queen said, "hasn't she? Tell me why."

Seven steadied herself. "You may be able to communicate with me while I'm regenerating, but I'm no longer a drone. I don't answer to you."

The Queen tilted her head. This was a common human gesture indicating thought, but for the Borg Queen it was a command. A freefloating viewscreen entered Seven's periphery and descended to a place where both she and the Queen could witness its picture. On it was a distant vision of *Voyager,* cruising at impulse speed, coming toward them.

"I've extrapolated *Voyager*'s trajectory. I know you're returning to the nebula. I suggest you alter course."

Perhaps while she was "here," Seven thought, she might graft information from the Queen. "Why should we comply?"

"You've always been my favorite, Seven." The Queen regarded her with eyes like ballbearings. True to her reputation, she was too clever to answer a question so directly. "And, in spite of their obvious imperfections, I know how much you care about the *Voyager*'s crew. So I've left them alone. Imagine how you'd feel if I were forced to assimilate them."

Seven locked eyes with the Queen. Anger rose in her.

123

"*Voyager* is no threat to the Collective. We simply want to return to the Alpha Quadrant."

"And I have no objection to that. But if you try to enter my nebula again, I'll destroy you."

To prove her point, she tilted her head again.

Bolts of silver-green energy crackled through Seven's alcove, breaking across her body and mind. She tried to move her hands, her legs, to step out of the neuroelectrical storm. This was the Queen's warning, to fry the mind of her enemies if they wished to remain enemies. Be assimilated or be cooked alive.

Pain raged through Seven's existence until she no longer remembered her name.

Sparks carried her back to the brighter place where she had begun. She remembered something about this place, but could not put a name to it. Convulsions thundered through her muscles. Hard gray flooring came up to slap her, and she lay still.

She heard only the buzz of her blood and the voice of the computer.

"Warning: regenerative cycle incomplete. Warning . . ."

"Her cortical node was exposed to a low-energy electromagnetic surge. It could've been much worse."

The Doctor made his report, but neither Captain Janeway nor Admiral Janeway took much comfort in what they had just been told. Seven lay on a biobed, looking worn and even frightened.

Captain Janeway took this as the first sign of things going mightily wrong.

"What happened to you, Seven?" she asked. Her voice was stern and her throat rough with tension.

"It was the Borg Queen," Seven reported. "She wanted to

make sure I'd be able to deliver a message. She said she'd assimilate *Voyager* if we attempted to reenter this nebula."

None of that made much sense. The Queen could assimilate them any time she wanted to, considering that she had forty-seven cubes within striking distance of the ship at this very moment. In all reality, there would be nothing, nothing, and nothing that could be done to stop her. The second fact, that *Voyager* was on its way back to the nebula, running directly into the swarm, was another contributing worry. They were heading to give the Queen even more advantage, if that were possible.

"Why's it so important to her?"

"It doesn't matter," Admiral Janeway interrupted. "She's not going to be able to make good on her threat."

Janeway turned to her, suddenly stern. "I wish I shared your confidence."

"You would, if you had as much experience with the Queen as I've had."

Oh, such statements! That was a *big* damned statement.

She shook her head. "It was one thing to attempt this when we thought it was a secret. But if the Borg are monitoring us—"

The admiral cut her off. "There's no guarantee they won't try to assimilate *Voyager* even if we don't go back into the nebula."

"Is that supposed to be reassuring?"

"I'm not saying the Borg aren't dangerous," the admiral insisted, "but from my perspective, they're thirty years behind the times!"

"We shouldn't push our luck."

"Luck's not going to have anything to do with it. I know you don't want to hear too much about the future, but I ran into the Borg a few more times before I made it home. If I hadn't developed technology and tactics that could defeat them, I wouldn't be standing here today."

Would I?

The older woman's unspoken question irritated the captain even more because she heard it in her own head. These professions of superiority were beginning to sound trumped up. The admiral could posture and puff all she wanted, but she was from a future that *hadn't* gone into the nebula with forty-seven Borg cubes inside. She might think she had already experienced everything, but this one would be new even for her.

Captain Janeway resisted pointing that out, mostly because she didn't want her crew to lose what little confidence they had.

"We'll maintain course for the nebula," she said. Silently she added *for now,* and hoped the admiral picked up on the tail end of the message. "But we'll stay at red alert. And I want continuous scans for Borg activity."

"Aye, captain," Seven responded. Eagerly she got off the biobed.

"We'll need to find a way," Janeway added, "to modify your alcove so the Queen can't hurt you again."

"I can help with that," said her counterpart with a smile.

"There's no substitute for experience," she added.

Red alert. The astrometrics lab flashed with warning lights. The domescreen's focus was at maximum readiness, displaying a starchart. The starcharts of the Delta Quadrant would be one of the little perks of this whole years-long problem. *Voyager* would bring back—or send back—the paths through otherwise uncharted territory.

Chakotay hurried in, but at the last moment forced himself to quell his agitation. He strode quickly to Seven, who was busy with the admiral's conversions. She looked well enough, but electromagnetics were nothing to play with, never mind the Borg Queen's vindictive manipulation.

"I heard what happened," he began without greeting. "Are you all right?"

"I'm fine," she said. She didn't look at him.

She was self-conscious, he could tell, probably worried not so much about herself, but that she might provide a conduit for the Borg Queen to infiltrate *Voyager.*

He tried to distract her with some mundane silliness. "Because if you need time to rest," he said, "I'm in charge of the duty roster."

Would she get the joke? Nobody played with duty rosters while a ship was on alert status. Maybe she didn't know that yet.

"It would be inappropriate to allow our personal relationship to affect your command decision."

Was she smiling? Almost?

Chakotay got the feeling she was getting the better of him. "You're right," he murmured. "This is a time to keep things professional. So give me a report."

"There's no sign of Borg activity within a ten-light-year radius."

"That's good news, crewman."

She turned to him and suspended the effort to be icy. "Yes, sir . . . but we shouldn't underestimate the Collective."

"The admiral seems pretty confident we can get past them."

"*Captain* Janeway is more cautious."

"Our chances," Chakotay said, "would be good with *one* Kathryn Janeway on the bridge. But with two? I'd bet on this ship any day. If we do make it back to Earth . . . what are your plans?"

Seven's enormous eyes grew misty and tightened slightly. Chakotay got the idea she hadn't made any plans, hadn't really absorbed the idea of getting back to their common homeworld, simply because she had never expected these things to occur which might shorten their trip by so much.

"I assume," she began tentatively, "Starfleet will want to debrief me. And then, I suppose, I'll attempt to find a useful position somewhere." She looked up at him and they passed a charged moment together. "You?"

Chakotay shrugged, and touched her chin with one finger. "I don't know yet either. But wherever I end up . . . I'm going to make sure it's within transporter range of you."

Tom Paris had never seen so much activity on the engineering deck. He went there to chase his wife, who shouldn't even be on duty, never mind flogging dozens of crewmen into hurrying with what amounted to alien technology being fitted into *Voyager*'s systems. Even as he stepped through the doors, he could tell she was overdoing—even before he saw her. He could hear her voice snap through the air.

"I don't want the whole system crashing because of one faulty relay. Install new ones!"

"Yes, ma'am," some poor schlock responded.

Paris paused and shook his head. Usually it was hard to believe there were more than ten people on the ship, never mind most of them crowded into one deck, running around with parts and installation tools and enviro-suits, practically crawling on top of each other. Add to that the idea that his wife could bark them all into quivering submission while carrying their child— and some men thought *their* lives were weird.

"And I need an update on the inductor capacitance—"

"B'Elanna . . ."

"This time don't make me wait more than five minutes. I have to report to the captain *and* to the admiral. My least favorite re-port is 'I don't know yet, ma'am.' Clear?"

"B'Elanna, this is your husband calling . . . anybody home?" Paris strode up to her and tilted into her periphery.

"Shouldn't you be on the bridge?" she snapped.

He pulled her to a more secluded area and fielded the glances of the busy crewmen hurrying around them. "Is there something wrong with the pilot's requesting a systems report from the chief engineer?"

"The last report I got was that the comm system was working perfectly."

"Okay, you caught me," he admitted with a shrug. "I'm check-ing up on you."

What kind of husband would he be if he didn't? Red alert and all, Borg cubes, nebulae, admirals . . . Maybe the two of them should settle down on some nice asteroid with their baby, build a cottage, plant a garden, and tell the captain to just come back for them through some other temporal notch later on.

"I'm fine," she said, managing a halfhearted smile. His con-cern seemed to ease her clutter of concerns and frustrations.

"Your back?"

"I'm ignoring it."

"I'd offer you a massage, but then eveyone would probably want one."

The smile broadened. "You know," she murmured, "for a Starfleet flyboy, you're pretty sweet."

Paris returned the smile. Now that he had managed to relax her a little, he glanced around at all the work happening around them. "So how's it going?"

She shook her head in admiration. "This armor technology the admiral brought—it's incredible! I hate to sound like Harry, but we might actually make it this time."

Paris took note of her words, but what he really paid attention to was her tone. "Why don't you seem happy about that?" he asked.

"I am happy . . . it's just . . . I'd gotten used to the idea of raising the baby on *Voyager.* But now . . . I might end up delivering her at Starfleet Medical instead of sickbay."

As he watched her expression, his shoulders sagged a little. Boy, this was one schizophrenic crew. Sometimes they wanted to go home, sometimes they were already home—

"That wouldn't be so bad, would it?" he pursued.

"Not as long as you're there with me. And I want the Doctor. Not some stranger."

"You'd have to take him off-line to keep him away."

When faced with the facts of how many people truly cared about them and their baby, maybe the idea that she was giving birth on behalf of the whole ship's complement, B'Elanna smiled again, this time more sincerely. "If we do make it home, where do you think we'll live?"

"We can always stay with my parents for a while—ooooh, you're right. Bad idea."

"Of course," she said, "it probably doesn't matter to you anyway. You flyboys are all the same. You'll probably take the first piloting assignment that comes along and leave me to change diapers."

He grinned at the idea—not of leaving, but of his half-Klingon wife patting powder on a little moon. "Not a chance."

"Come in."

Kathryn Janeway hardly noticed the door chime until it rang

for the third time. She was bent over her desk monitor, reviewing graphic after graphic of Borg cubes. As if it helped . . .

She knew the cubes well enough from the inside as well as out, yet somehow they just got more complicated, not less, like a swamp that was ever-changing.

When she finally looked up, aware that someone had entered, she found not a yeoman or Chakotay or anybody she particularly wanted to see, but Admiral Janeway standing there like a ghost.

A ghost with a dinner tray.

"What's this?" Janeway asked.

"Crewman Chell told me you skipped lunch. I'm not about to let you miss dinner too."

Oh, fine. She not only had a double—she had a granny. The absurd solicitousness just made her mad. "Thanks, but I don't have time."

"You're going to have to make some. You're too thin."

Janeway sat back and regarded the echo of herself over there. "It just hit me . . . I'm going to turn into my mother."

The admiral lifted the cover off the tray. "I make a better pot roast than she ever did. I hope you don't mind—I invited a friend to join us."

"Good afternoon, ladies."

Chakotay.

Janeway watched him stride into the room. The admiral was gazing at him in that same odd nostalgic way she had addressed Seven. Another clue?

Her first officer made himself comfortable on the couch beside Admiral Janeway. They looked odd together—so many years apart in age—and yet there was a connection.

"How are my two favorite ladies this fine day?" he asked merrily.

"You're such a liar," the admiral accused. "How much do you think you can put over on me, Chakotay?"

His cheeks flushed with a touch of color. He crossed his legs and pretended to relax. "It's all a test to reveal your real identity."

"You mean to see whether or not I have a cape and a big red 'J' under my uniform?"

"Something like that."

"Why don't you just ask me some key questions that only our friend here and I would know?" The admiral gestured to the captain, then almost immediately seemed to think she'd been rude. "Sorry, Captain. I don't mean to speak about you as if you're not here."

Janeway came around her desk and accepted a cup of coffee. "Oh, don't mind me. I'm just a fifth wall."

"I'll take the bet," Chakotay said. "Admiral, why don't you tell us some things that only *you* would know?"

"The captain prefers I don't discuss the future."

"Oh, it doesn't matter now, does it?" Janeway stated. "After all, we're about to wipe it out, whatever it is. At least, we *hope* we are. How confident are you that after today none of your memories will have happened at all?"

The admiral dropped her smug expression. So she wasn't as secure as she sounded, was she?

"Like what?" she asked.

The odd dinner meeting dissolved rather quickly from information into reminiscence. And bizarre it was indeed, given that the ship was at red alert, emergency status, enemy-in-sight, and under conversion for critical new systems that would never have a chance to be shaken down. Everything could explode in their faces—literally.

"What about the first contact with the Rotenians?" Chakotay asked, the tenth in a roster of questions. He had been the one to keep the conversation ever moving forward.

"How could I forget?" the admiral uttered.

Captain Janeway nodded at the shared memory. "Now, they *were* telepaths." She glanced at Chakotay. "How many days did it take to negotiate passage through their space?"

"Twelve," the admiral answered before Chakotay had the chance—something she'd done several times now, and it tended to relax them all.

"Whenever I tried to bluff them," Janeway added, "that annoying little diplomat would say, 'I know what you're thinking, Captain . . .' "

Chakotay laughed. "Until the morning you marched into his office and said—"

"Tell me what I'm thinking *now!*" both women chimed.

All three laughed, but the two voices, in perfect pitch with each other, inflections, volume, everything, made Chakotay shake his head. "Am I the only one who thinks this is a little strange?"

The captain reserved her comment and hid her edginess in the mundane. "More tea?"

Admiral Janeway nodded and said, "Thank you."

When the captain got up and left, the admiral watched her go to the other side of the room. She knew the captain was only pretending to be so relaxed, hoping to ply more information out of an admiral less on her guard. They weren't so good at fooling each other, but the older officer had the advantage of time and knowledge. She leaned toward Chakotay and lowered her voice to a whisper.

"How's your personal life?" she asked pointedly.

"Admiral?"

"There's no need to be coy with me, Chakotay. I know exactly what's going on." When Chakotay shot a glance at the captain, Admiral Janeway quickly said, "Don't worry. She doesn't know yet. So how are things going with Seven?"

Chakotay's eyes narrowed with suspicion, but he smiled. "Great."

She was giving herself away in what could be the wrong way. Hinting at their personal future might ruin everything. Still, to see him so happy—to see him at all . . .

"Helm to Captain Janeway."

The admiral perked up and almost answered Tom Paris's call to action, but the younger Captain Janeway beat her to it.

"Janeway. What is it?"

"We're coming within short-range sensors of the nebula, Captain."

Paris sounded cautious, maybe even nervous. Of course— he would be. He was about to become a father, and didn't know whether his baby would live one day, or a hundred years.

The captain cast the admiral one glance, and their relationship shifted back to the hard-edged thing it had been an hour ago.

"Batten and secure the ship. All hands to battle stations. Prepare to engage the Borg. I'll be right there, Tom." Janeway turned to face both the admiral and Chakotay, who got to his feet quickly when she said, "Dinner's over."

They followed her to the bridge, where the mood was already tense. Within literally seconds, Tuvok, Kim, and Seven arrived to take their bridge posts, and there was now a full contingent of the ship's senior officers in this one small space, including a Starfleet admiral.

Captain Janeway took her command chair, a gesture not lost on everyone around her—and she noticed their quick attentions.

The admiral came to stand behind her. A power play? Not subtle enough.

"Janeway to engineering. Are we ready with the admiral's armor modifications?"

B'Elanna Torres's voice came up through the comm system complete with its thready strain. *"None of this has been tested, Captain. Can't we stall for a day?"*

"You know better than that, B'Elanna. Give me a green light as soon as you can have all systems on-line. We're approaching the nebula, and you know what they say . . . there's no time like a present."

Zing. She avoided a glance at the admiral.

After a few moments of clicking and waiting, B'Elanna said, *"Go ahead, Captain."*

Janeway drew a breath and let it out slowly. If the Borg didn't know they were here yet, they would in a minute.

"Deploy armor," she ordered.

The hull drummed with hammering noises as plates of armor shot around the ship to seal the hull. It was a sound none of them had ever heard, and once again Janeway got a feeling of resentment for what the admiral knew that she did not. The ship was a knight now, heading to the lists.

Janeway gazed at the encompassing mustard-colored fume on the main screen.

"All right, Mr. Paris," she said. "Enter the nebula."

CHAPTER 14

CUBE!

The Borg found them instantly, were waiting for them, but Janeway expected such a reception and would've been foolish not to. At the moment she first saw the approaching cube, with three of its sides fully visible and one angry point heading toward the starship, a surge of nauseous regret bolted up from her guts and almost knocked her out of her chair. She had allowed herself to trust a person who might be an illusion. Even if the admiral were what she appeared to be, she could still turn out to be a demented radical from the future. Janeway had been lulled into trusting the admiral because she wanted to believe her mind would be strong and pure at that age—but . . .

The moment had come to live with her decision and let her doubts play out, to life or to death.

The cube was massive and stunning—always, every time they laid eyes on a Borg cube, the sight shocked. That a straight-edged block so simple and basic could be packed with technology somehow defied style and convention. If not the nemesis to individuality it was, the Borg cube could be a work of art.

Voyager was attacked instantly, blows that would ordinarily have sent her spinning.

Janeway braced for the worst and looked at Tuvok with her unspoken question.

"Armor integrity at ninety-seven percent," he said over the thrum of strikes and the ship's trembling.

Chakotay caught the captain's eye and they shared a moment of awe. Then Janeway eyed the admiral, who betrayed a little smile of satisfaction.

"Evasive, Mr. Paris," Janeway said, keeping a grip on her role here. "We're not here to engage them. Let's have full impulse speed on our heading. Ignore the cubes."

Easy to say, and in fact critical now as two more cubes were born from the fumes of the inner nebula to join in pursuit. *Voyager* rolled past them and engaged in a race to the death.

"Tuvok?"

"Integrity holding at ninety percent."

She gripped her armrests. "Maintain course!"

The shaking suddenly stopped, replaced by giant green scanning beams washing over the ship's hull.

The admiral checked a console and nodded as if to herself. "They're looking for ways to adapt," she said. Clearly she expected this.

Janeway cast her a glance and started to speak, but her intentions were swallowed as the Borg cubes all fired at once and the ship shook violently.

"They're firing simultaneously!" Chakotay called over the noise. "Focusing on a single section!"

An alarm went off on Tuvok's station. "Port armor integrity down to fifty percent!" he called. "Forty percent!"

The whine was deafening.

"Mr. Paris, attack pattern alpha-one!" Janeway ordered. "Target lead cub and fire transphasic torpedoes."

They heard the armor split apart, exposing a launch mechanism. If only it would work! Untested, unproven—

The nebula lit up. Torpedoes blew free of their housings and collided with the first Borg cube. Janeway expected something a little better than the usual *poof* of smoke and sparks against the cube's outer mechanicals. She got much more.

An explosion of a level met only by the collisions of spatial bodies rocked through the nebula, washing *Voyager* up on her nacelles and blowing the other two cubes back the way they'd come.

Bright white clouds edged with neon green made an enormous gouted fireball behind the ship, then another, and another.

The cube had exploded!

Exploded!

Well, damn—the admiral was a nice little old lady after all!

If only they could see the look on the Borg Queen's face right now! A blown-up cube!

Janeway kept her head. "Target the second cube."

The second hit was as effective as the first. The next cube broke through the fireball of the first, only to be struck corner-on with the starship's second salvo.

Possibly because of proximity, the second explosion was more ghastly and glorious than the first.

"The third cube is retreating!" Harry Kim shouted, overcome with whatever he was feeling.

Disbelief, probably. Such untempered joy was rarely the profit of *Voyager*'s contacts with the Borg or anyone else. There were always costs.

At this moment, though, everything went their way and they were soaring!

"Distance to the center?" Chakotay asked.

"Less than one hundred thousand kilometers," Seven answered instantly.

On her last word the ship blew out of the gassy wall of the nebula into a clear center, a huge area of empty space fenced off all around by more thousands of cubic kilometers of poisoned yellow vapor.

Voyager became tiny again. Not because of the clearing or the vapor, but because of the structure turning before her. Before them in space hung a Borg colossus, a pinwheel of Olympian proportions spreading its extensions out, out, out beyond the range of the sensors to bring to the screen. Like some elephantine toy made of a billions pieces, the pinwheel might as well have been a display of fireworks gone solid and with a crust of circuitry bolted on every inch. At the end of each conduit was a glowing transwarp aperture held open by huge struts.

No one had ever before seen such a gargantuan structure—or such was the bet Captain Janeway made with herself, despite the presence of her future self, who clearly was not so surprised. Yet even the admiral stared with rekindled awe.

"What the hell is it?" Janeway demanded in a warning tone.

"Mr. Paris," the admiral said instead, "alter course to enter the aperture at coordinates three-four-six by four-two!"

"Belay that!" the captain snapped. "I asked you a question! What *is* it?"

"The road home."

"It's more than that," Seven broke in. "It's a transwarp hub."

Janeway's memory awakened with a jolt. "You told me once there were only six of them in the galaxy—"

"That's correct," Seven responded.

The captain swung to the admiral. "You knew this was here, but you didn't tell me! Why?"

"I'll answer all your questions once we're back in the Alpha Quadrant."

"Take us out of this nebula!"

Paris turned to them both. "Captain?"

"You heard me."

"I gave you an order, Lieutenant," the admiral barked. "Proceed to aperture—"

"This is my bridge, Admiral," Janeway interrupted, "and I'll have you removed if necessary. Mr. Paris, take us out!"

They had to hit warp speed to clear the nebula without being killed. Their victory over the two Borg cubes had been quickly slapped down by the sight of the pinwheel, the transwarp hub that so thoroughly dwarfed them, the cubes, and their place in the galaxy. If the Borg had these profound mammoths around the galaxy, then the Federation was already beaten. It was just a matter of time.

Such was the sour attitude in the astrometrics lab as Seven of Nine described to them the replay of what they had seen and now recorded. Even the image of the hub created a gut-wrenching fear and frustration.

140

The admiral hovered in the background, her arms folded tightly across her body. She was angry.

Janeway didn't care. She would have honesty and completeness, if nothing else.

Seven had to reduce the magnification six times before the whole hub would even let itself be seen on the large dome-screen.

"This hub connects with thousands of transwarp conduits with endpoints in all four quadrants," Seven explained. "It allows the Collective to deploy vessels almost anywhere in the galaxy within minutes."

As every heart sank—with the possible exception of the admiral's—Tuvok added, "Of all the Borg's tactical advantages, this could be the most significant."

"It's no wonder," Chakotay said, "the Queen didn't want us in that nebula."

"So how do we destroy it?" Janeway demanded.

She shocked them with this question, but she didn't care. So it was a *big* mission. So what? What else was this ship for?

The admiral reacted, but Janeway paid her no attention. Whether she liked the idea or not remained a mystery.

Seven worked her controls and changed the image to display one of the high-tech struts in close-up. "The structure is supported by a series of interspatial manifolds. If we could disable enough of them, theoretically the hub would collapse."

Oh, that *really* sounded too easy. Still, it also sounded possible. With the explanation came the thousand questions, primary of which was—why hadn't anybody tried it before?

Or maybe somebody had.

"This is a waste of time," the admiral ground out from behind them. "The shielding for those manifolds is regulated from the central nexus, by the Queen herself. You might be able to damage one of them, maybe two, but by the time you move on to the third, she'd adapt."

The captain wasn't annoyed enough to ignore good information, but suggested, "There may be a way to bring them down simultaneously."

"From where? *Inside* the hub? *Voyager* would be crushed like a bug."

Chakotay got between them before Janeway responded. "What about taking the conduit back to the Alpha Quadrant, and then destroying the structure from the other side."

"This hub is here," the admiral caustically chided. "There's nothing in the Alpha Quadrant but exit apurtures. While you're all standing around dreaming up fantasy tactical scenarios, the Queen is studying her scans of our armor and weapons. And she's probably got the entire Collective working on a way to counter them. Take the ship back to the nebula and go home before it's too late."

Before she said anything else, Janeway reached out and grasped the older woman's arm. To Chakotay and Seven, Tuvok and everything within her power, she ordered, "Find a way to destroy that hub." To the admiral, she said, "Let's take a walk."

"I want to know why you didn't tell me about this."

Admiral Janeway didn't react to the captain's question in any outward manner, but simply walked beside Janeway as they pointlessly emerged from the astrometrics lab and left the officers with their awesome task.

"Because I remember how stubborn and self-righteous I used to be," the senior officer said, "and I figured you might try to do something stupid."

The captain bristled. "We have an opportunity to deal a crippling blow to the Borg. It could save billions of lives!"

"I didn't spend the last ten years looking for a way to get this crew home earlier just so you could throw it all away on some intergalactic goodwill mission."

Disgusted, Janeway stopped walking and faced her, faced the sickening image of a captain gone sour, a promoted ponce who had forgotten why decent people rose up and made starships, and why only a handful among them were chosen to command.

"Maybe we should go back to sickbay," she rasped.

"Why? So you can have me sedated?"

"So I can have the Doctor reconfirm your identity. I refuse to believe I'll ever become as cynical as you."

The admiral wasn't insulted. "Am I the only one experiencing déjà vu here?"

"What are you talking about?"

"Seven years ago, you had a chance to use the Caretaker's Array to get *Voyager* home. But instead, you destroyed it."

Janeway stood back a step. Did she really have to explain? Did she have to remind this shriveled soul that a captain's first duty is to the bigger picture, and that everybody on a starship signed up with the vow of giving his or her life to the betterment of those who had supplied them with this power and authority? That this ship wasn't a toy or a private plane?

"I did what I knew was right," she proclaimed.

"You chose to put the lives of strangers ahead of the lives of your crew," the admiral said caustically. "You can't make the same mistake again."

Janeway's stomach rolled to think this person was even related to her, never mind the reality. The lives of strangers? What was that supposed to mean? No ship exists *just* to protect the lives of those aboard!

Her jaw set hard. She battled down the wish to fight. "You got *Voyager* home," she said. "That means I will too. If it takes a few more years, then that's—"

"Seven of Nine is going to die."

"What?"

"Three years from now. She'll be injured on an away mission. She'll make it back to *Voyager,* and die in the arms of her husband."

"Husband?"

"Chakotay."

Janeway felt her innards buckle. Was the admiral making this up just to get a rise out of her? The other woman was tricky—Janeway intimately knew just how tricky.

Yet there was a hardness of truth in the admiral's eyes. "He'll never be the same after Seven's death. And neither will you."

Janeway tried to let this sink in. She was also obligated to cling to her oath—that the life of no single crewman would stand in the way of the ship's primary mission to protect life and peace and stability on a much grander scale than these decks.

"If I know what's going to happen," she attempted, "I can avoid it."

"Seven's not the only one," the admiral shot again. "Between this day and the day I got *Voyager* home, I lost twenty-two crew members. And then, of course, there's Tuvok."

"What about him?" Janeway snapped.

The admiral swaggered as she shifted her feet. "You're forgetting the Temporal Prime Directive, Captain—"

"To hell with it!"

"Fine. Tuvok has a degenerative neurological condition that he hasn't told you about."

How many punches could one rib cage take?

"There's a cure in the Alpha Quadrant," the admiral went on harshly. "Even if you alter *Voyager*'s route, limit your contact with alien species, you're going to lose people. But I'm offering you a chance to get them all home safe and sound—today! Are you really going to walk away from that?"

CHAPTER 15

"YOUR CONCERN IS APPRECIATED, CAPTAIN, BUT PREMATURE. IT will be several years before the symptoms become serious. Until then, the Doctor can manage my condition with medication."

Kathryn Janeway listened to Tuvok's polite protestations and took everything with a grain of salt. Tuvok didn't incline toward deception, but even keeping his condition from her had been a kind of lie. She knew he was thinking more of her than himself—after all, she couldn't exactly dismiss him from the Service on a medical discharge, could she?

"Is it true," she asked, "what the admiral said? That there's a cure in the Alpha Quadrant?"

Tuvok was obviously disturbed by her knowing this information and sagged a little. "It's called a *fal-tor-voh*. And it requires a mind-meld with another Vulcan."

"What about the other Vulcans on *Voyager?*" The question sounded flat just as she finished it. He would've thought of that possibility first off.

"None of them is compatible," he pointed out politely.

"But members of your family are," she inferred. "If you knew that returning to the Alpha Quadrant was your only chance for recovery, why didn't you object when I asked you to find a way to destroy the hub?"

It was almost an insult to ask him that. Unlike Admiral Janeway, Tuvok was still a Starfleet officer first and a member of an adopted family second.

"My sense of logic isn't impaired yet," he said. He seemed never to have considered his own well-being in balance with the lives of innocent possible Borg victims—and he was right not to. "If we succeed, billions of lives will be saved."

Janeway dismissed the ship, the crew, the universe, for just a moment. "What about your life?"

Sanguine, Tuvok had accepted the noblest route. "To quote Ambassador Spock . . . 'The needs of the many outweigh the needs of the few.' "

There was a great lesson here, one Janeway had almost allowed to slip away. Yes, the Alpha Quadrant sooner than later held many temptations, but they weren't just children lost in the woods with no one to worry about other than themselves. She was suddenly ashamed of Admiral Janeway and disappointed that the crew had met the woman she might become.

The woman she might *have* become. She could change things now. If Admiral Janeway stayed on *Voyager* for the rest of her life, she and the captain would be separate people, and the captain was not obligated to turn into this other woman.

And I won't. I won't become her. I don't admire her. She has special knowledge, but she's forgotten why intelligent beings seek knowledge and reach out with it.

She looked at Tuvok, and vowed that he would be her example, the sentinel for *Voyager*'s unwritten future.

"I appreciate your candor, Admiral, but Captain Janeway is my commanding officer. I won't disobey her."

Seven of Nine accepted the admiral's disturbing news with almost as much distaste as the admiral's bitter suggestion. Betray the captain?

"I'm not asking you to," the admiral said, pursuing Seven back to the freestanding console. "I simply want you to tell her that in your opinion, destroying the hub is too risky, the cost is too high—"

"I can't do that."

The admiral held out a hand. "Even if it means avoiding the consequences I mentioned?"

Seven quelled a particularly human sense of vulnerability. "Now that I know about those consequences, they're no longer a certainty. But even if they were, my death would be a small price to pay for the destruction of the transwarp network."

The admiral watched her work, watched her try to lock herself into the course of action the captain wanted, a course that would sacrifice her chance for a long life with Chakotay—such a strange and wondrous possibility! Seven was not as practiced at logic under conflict as Mr. Tuvok, but she tried.

"I've known you for a long time, Seven," the admiral attempted. "Longer than you've known yourself. You're thinking that collapsing the network would be an opportunity to atone for atrocities you participated in while you were a drone."

Seven's shoulders tightened. Her nerves seemed to be suddenly burning from the inside out. These had been atrocious indeed, the things she had been forced to do, the crimes against life, against freedom and choice, love and diversity of pursuit. The thoughts of atonement had always been private, small thoughts lost within her search for individuality, but they were there and she had entertained them.

Wasn't it called revenge?

Perhaps it was more complicated than simple revenge. She owed something to the galaxy.

"It's time to let go of the past," the admiral pressed on, "and start thinking about your future!"

"My future," Seven forced out, "is insignificant compared to the lives of the people we'd be saving."

"You're being selfish."

"Selfish? I'm talking about helping others—"

"Strangers. In a hypothetical scenario. I'm talking about real life! Your colleagues . . . your friends . . . the people who love you! Imagine the impact your death would have on them!"

Seven paused and gazed into the eyes of this person, this *stranger.* If these choices and decisions were part of being human, then she had reached a new level.

"Excuse me, Admiral," she said bluntly. "I have work to complete."

She remained otherwise very still. She stood her philosophical ground, waited for the admiral to digest the expression in her eyes and to leave the lab. Once alone, Seven turned back to the purpose she would not abandon for her own edification, and to the populations unnamed who needed her to be bigger than herself.

And she was proud. Frightened, proud. A strong and useful combination.

Everybody rallied to the captain's plan. To the last of *Voyager*'s crew, even B'Elanna and Tom Paris, who were about to become parents, were willing to make good on their promise to be higher than themselves, for the good of a galaxy that desperately needed heroes.

In the shadow of the irritated and greatly subdued admiral, Captain Janeway found herself puffed up with pride. She knew the admiral had been lobbying the crew, and she knew what response they had unilaterally given.

The briefing room was now cluttered with coffee cups, water glasses, padds and people. They had spread out to their various stations, analyzed every last possibility, and come together to a single purpose like a cluster of surgeons about to operate on the same patient.

Janeway sat next to Chakotay. Around the table were Paris, B'Elanna, Kim, the Doctor, Tuvok, and Seven, and over there, apart, was Admiral Janeway. Tuvok had a graphic of the transwarp hub playing on the monitor. Even small and transparent, the monstrosity was frightening.

"Once inside," Tuvok was reporting, "we'd fire a spread of transphasic torpedoes."

Seven added, "They'd be programmed to detonate simultaneously."

"If the torpedoes penetrate the shielding, the conduits should begin to collapse in a cascade reaction."

Janeway drew a breath to clear her head. This had been a long meeting after a tiring day. The explanation-sharing was giving her whiplash. She wished they'd all report to one person and that person would just say everything at once instead of the zigzag dialogue. The irony was not lost on her that this attack was only possible because of technology that Admiral Janeway had brought from the future, and they were using it to go very much against the admiral's purpose.

ENDGAME

"In order to avoid the shock wave," Tuvok continued as the graphic began its theoretical collapse, "we'd have less than ten seconds to exit the hub."

What more could be said? The plan could be executed, could succeed, or could be their glorious last couple of minutes. Their legend would die with them. No one would really know why.

Billions of lives. Whole planets out there trying to live and thrive, most not even knowing they were percolating fodder for the Borg. If the encompassing plan for assimilation continued on its extrapolated path, someday there would be nothing in the galaxy but Borgified life-forms. True, there would be no more death in the conventional sense. But there would also be no more life, no love or ambition, no striving for betterment, no failing and getting up from failure, no new greatness, no new dreams.

Worth doing?

Janeway gripped the arms of her chair. "A long time ago," she began solemnly, "I made a decision that stranded this crew in the Delta Quadrant. I don't regret that decision. But I didn't know all of you then, and *Voyager* was just a starship. It's much more than that now. It's become our home."

She paused, to see if this very odd statement would have some effect on them. The only response, though, was Tuvok's brow when she uttered the uninspiring phrase "just a starship."

Maybe she should stop baiting them.

"I know I could order you to carry out this plan," she went on, more mellow than before, less posturing. "None of you would hesitate for a second. But I'm not going to do that. You know the crewmen who work under you, and you know what your own hearts are telling you. So we're not going to attempt this unless everyone in this room agrees. No one will think less of you if you don't."

To whom was she lying? Herself? Possibly. To them? No—

they knew she already understood the answer they would give. This was all a weird performance, all for the admiral's sake— just so *she* would never again interfere.

"Captain?" Harry Kim spoke up, probably not understanding the game Janeway was playing.

No, of course he wasn't picking up on her subtle trick. Janeway gazed warmly at him, at his innocence, and in his boyish features and his guileless eyes she saw the myriad souls they were about to attempt to save.

"Go ahead, Harry," she accepted.

He hesitated, formulating his thoughts. "I think it's safe to say that no one on this crew has been more obsessed with getting home than I have. But when I think of everything we've been through together, maybe it's not the destination that matters . . . maybe it's the journey." He paused again, and made contact with each of them at the table. "I can't think of any place I'd rather be, or any people I'd rather be with."

His words hung in the air a moment, then drifted into the coffee cup Tom Paris held up in front of him.

"To the journey," Paris declared.

One by one their raised their glasses or cups, and to the last echoed the sentiment of solidarity, admiral or no admiral, Borg or no Borg.

Off watch, at red alert. The two were contradictory. Nobody was off watch at red alert, yet Captain Janeway stood in the mess hall alone, near the window, reviewing a padd and sipping another cup of coffee. It was her tenth in the past couple of hours. She'd either float away or just use up all they had left. Maybe that was why she eventually "gave it up." Wasn't any left.

"Coffee, black."

She turned at the sound of her own voice. The admiral was here. When had she come in?

A cup of coffee was dispensed from the replicator. The admiral took it and approached her.

"I thought you gave it up," Janeway commented.

The admiral offered a very familiar shrug with just a tip of her head. "I've decided to revive a few of my old habits."

"Oh? What else, besides the coffee?"

Admiral Janeway's eyes twinkled at the irony. "Well . . . I used to be much more idealistic. I took a lot of risks."

What was she driving at? Janeway deliberately didn't say anything, letting her silence propel the moment.

"I've been so determined to get my crew home," the admiral regretfully went on, "for so many years . . . I forgot how much they loved being together. And I forgot how loyal they were to . . . you." She paced a few steps, then went on. "It's taken me a few days to realize it, but this is your ship, your crew. Not mine. I was wrong to lie to you, to think I could talk you out of something you'd set your mind to—"

"You were only doing what you thought was right for all of us." Janeway cut her off with a platitude. She really didn't want to hear any more.

"Well, you've changed my mind about that," the admiral said anyway. "And I'd like to help you carry out your mission. Maybe together we can increase our odds."

Janeway stared at her, unblinking, until her eyes hurt. Could it be this easy? Flip, flop, I'm with you now?

Or had the actions and devotions of the crew really had this much of an effect on a person whom she knew—damned well *knew*—was hardheaded and inflexible on items of conviction?

She couldn't read the admiral's eyes, despite the mirror effect. There was still a factor of possible manipulation going on. And she wanted to be cautious, to hold back her trust. She owed it to everyone to be circumspect and not plunge forward just because the admiral decided to play nice.

Why were they at odds? Why were they playing mental games and challenges of authority and will? There was something wrong about this, and there had to be some better way. A captain with a ship of this power, a crew of this diverse talent . . . there had to be something she hadn't imagined.

For the first time she opened her brain to the crazy wedge of chance that she had until now been pushing away for the safety of her crew.

"Maybe we can do more than that. There's got to be a way to have our cake and eat it too."

The admiral scowled a bit. "We can't destroy the hub *and* get *Voyager* home."

"Are you absolutely sure about that?"

Clearly the admiral had never thought this way. She had been too single-minded, and now reconsidered.

"There might be a way," she offered quietly. "I considered it once . . . but it seemed too risky."

For the first time they genuinely understood each other, and genuinely agreed.

Janeway actually smiled. "That was before you decided to revive your old habits."

The admiral smiled back and took a sip from her coffee cup. "I don't know why I ever gave this up."

The admiral checked the readings at the helm of her shuttle when the captain entered, carrying a hypospray. Risky? This was

beyond the definition. They had, however, committed themselves and neither was looking back.

"It's about time." She looked up at the younger version of herself and saw the beginnings of lines around the eyes that had by
now become familiar and in a way reassuring. "I'm not getting
any younger, you know."

Janeway adjusted the hypo, then injected the admiral while
casually chiding, "You're sure you want to do this?"

"No, but *Voyager* isn't big enough for the both of us."

Somehow it was easy to joke, now that the critical, crazy decision had been made.

Didn't matter—if the captain succeeded in taking the ship
back to the Alpha Quadrant, then the admiral wouldn't exist anyway because the future would have been changed. If they didn't
succeed, well—there was no future to worry about. So she might
as well go.

Captain Janeway was watching her. "Good luck, Admiral."

"You too," the admiral said, rather quickly. Then she added,
"Captain . . . I'm glad I got to know you again."

Destiny took over, on autopilot. The captain got up and simply
left. There was nothing more to say.

The admiral was glad of it. Enough talking. She launched the
shuttle from the starship's bay with a surge of nostalgia and
wondrous ease, and instantly went to warp on a heading for the
Borg nebula and the transwarp hub. She would cross a threshold,
and she would disappear from the screens on the starship.

It was time to live or die, or both.

CHAPTER 16

CHAKOTAY HURRIED INTO THE LAB AND TOOK SOME KIND OF UNEX-plainable relief at seeing Seven hard at work. That vision of her had become like an icon for him. If there was a statue of her forming in his mind, it involved her standing at the console, her long limbs tight, her hair glossy, her eyes fixed and determined, her fingers playing the board as if it were an extension of herself.

The whole ship's company was tense like that. The admiral who had given them a chance at a whole new kind of future was now off board and had disappeared into the transwarp hub's glowing aperture.

"Any word from the admiral?

Seven shook her head stiffly. Her tone was formal. "We lost contact as soon as she entered the hub."

Sir. She all but said it.

He tried again. "Did the Borg give her any trouble?"

"Her vessel was scanned by several cubes, but none approached her, sir."

Oh, there it was, the term of address that set them apart. He tried to strike up a little banter. "Are we keeping things professional today?"

"Yes, Commander."

He smiled, but almost immediately his smile faded. She wasn't looking at him. Not at all.

"You're not joking, are you?" he asked.

"No."

She moved away from him, to another console. She didn't have to do that.

He followed her. "Hey . . . what's wrong?"

"Nothing. I'm just busy."

"I think I've gotten to know you a little better than that," he attempted, but her expression didn't change or soften, or anything.

"I'd prefer it if you didn't speak to me as though we're on intimate terms."

A surge of anger warmed between them. "We *are* on intimate terms," he protested.

"Not anymore."

Chakotay bristled. "What the hell is going on?"

She still wouldn't meet his eyes. "I've decided to alter the parameters of our relationship."

"You mind telling me why?"

"We both have dangerous occupations," she began flimsily, forcing every word. "It's possible one of us could be seriously injured . . . or worse. I believe it's best to avoid emotional attachment."

It was that damned admiral. It had to be.

Chakotay drew a sharp breath. "Maybe you can just flip some Borg switch and shut down your emotions, but I can't."

Finally she turned to him. "I suggest you try. It will make things less difficult for you if any harm were to come to me."

He digested this almost immediately, because he already had his suspicions. "Why are you suddenly so concerned about that? Is there something I should know?"

Perhaps she could see in his eyes that he suspected, that he wasn't quite as dull as would be necessary for a person not to notice the changes since the admiral's appearance. They were tampering with the future, and Admiral Janeway had been talking to the crew.

"The admiral suggests"—she paused as he rolled his eyes with anger and anticipation—"that your feelings for me will cause you pain in the future. I can't allow that to happen."

He took hold of her arm as if to anchor them in the present, and in the flexibility of things to come. "Any relationship entails risk, Seven, and nobody can guarantee what's going to happen tomorrow. Not even an admiral from the future."

He wanted to launch into an explanation, chase down the simple fact that the future had been incurably altered the moment Admiral Janeway stepped on the ship. Just her very existence told them things they weren't supposed to know. Now everything would be different, like it or not, and that meant nothing was carved in stone anymore. The future she had left was gone and would never return in the form she recognized.

And she was gone anyway! She was gone, and they were alone again to take care of each other.

"The only certainty," he ventured, "is how we feel about each other here and now. If you think I'm going to let you end this because of what *might* happen, then you need to get to know *me* a little better."

He reached out for her. Nothing overt—just put his hand between them and didn't retract it.

Slowly, her fingers, implanted with their Borg components,

came to meet his. Together they dismissed the threats and warnings, fears and hauntings placed between them by the woman who talked about strangers, but was no more than one herself.

But for the two of them, there was only one future today, which they found in the strength of each other's eyes. This was the future for which, together, they would fight.

"If you say 'relax' one more time I'm gonna rip your holographic *head off!*"

Even the corridor outside sickbay rang with Tom Paris's lovely wife's melodic voice. As Paris rushed into sickbay, he heard the Doctor's response.

"I hope you don't intend to kiss your baby with that mouth."

He rounded the partition and expected to see the Doctor's holoprogram rearranged. "Tell me this isn't another false alarm."

The Doctor looked up. "This isn't another false alarm."

B'Elanna lay on a pallet in obvious discomfort, half sitting up. Her teeth were gritted, her features hardened, her whole body drumhead-tight. This was it.

"I can't believe it," Paris murmured.

She stared at him and moaned, "Believe it!"

"I might actually win . . ."

"WHAT?"

"The baby pool. I picked today, fifteen hundred hours—"

Her head dropped back for a moment of respite and annoyance. "I'm so glad I could accommodate you."

The Doctor came to the other side of the bed with a tray of medical instruments that didn't look very comforting at all.

"I wouldn't celebrate yet," he warned casually. "Klingon labor sometimes lasts several days—" B'Elanna's expression stopped him cold and encouraged a slight rearrangement of the other half of that sentence. "Of course . . . I'm sure that won't be the case here."

"Bridge to Lieutenant Paris," the captain's voice interrupted. *"We're about to get under way."*

Oh, not now! Suddenly Paris was hit with the full-face blunt force of why having families on ships wasn't really a great idea. To divide a crewman's mind this way couldn't come to anything good. On a ship, emotional distraction and confused priorities were a recipe for disaster. He was the most qualified helmsman for what they were about to do—nobody else could do as well, not even the captain or Chakotay. Should he give up this precious moment or should he go to the bridge and make sure his baby had the best chance to live more than two minutes? And could he concentrate once he got there?

His place was *here*—wasn't it?

"Go," B'Elanna said, reading his mind.

"But—"

"No buts, flyboy. If this mission's going to succeed, we need our best pilot at the helm. Don't worry—I've got the Doctor."

He hated the idea of leaving. What kind of job could he do at the helm, thinking about her down here giving birth without his support? He'd started something, and now he might not be able to make good on following through. She'd be doing this alone. He had promised they wouldn't do anything important alone— this was marriage, wasn't it? While he was here, he would want to be on the bridge. On the bridge, he would be thinking about what he was missing and the family he was trying to ignore.

"Is there a problem, Mr. Paris?"

"On my way, Captain."

What choice did he really have?

* * *

ENDGAME

"I don't know how you do it."

Admiral Janeway took great joy in the Borg Queen's shock as the bodiless woman's eyes shot open. The Queen was in her private alcove within the great metropolis of the Unicomplex. To the Queen's perception, the admiral stood only a few feet away. A good effect.

Getting the drop on the Borg Queen—mmm, felt great.

"All those voices talking at once. You must get terrible headaches."

The Queen's pasty face bent into a scowl and she tilted her head.

"If you're calling drones to assimilate me," the admiral told her, "don't bother."

"I don't need drones to assimilate you," the Queen warned.

She moved toward the admiral, raising a threatening hand, but the admiral didn't flinch. The Queen ejected an assimiliation tubule from her wrist, an ugly and invasive device that represented orderly chaos for millions of former-people.

The tubule seemed to pierce Admiral Janeway's throat, but the admiral enjoyed just standing there, unaffected. "I'm not actually here, 'Your Majesty.' "

Angry, the Queen retracted the tubule.

"I'm in your mind," the admiral clarified.

"How?" the Queen asked.

"I'm using a synaptic interface. If I were you, I wouldn't waste my time trying to trace the signal."

Ah, the joy of advantage. Wasn't this pleasant? The freedom to give away all her secrets and still win?

161

"For the moment," the admiral went out, "it's beyond your abilities."

The Queen's expression hardened. "What do you want?"

"To make a deal. 'Captain' Janeway thinks I'm here to help her destroy your transwarp network."

"That's beyond *your* abilities."

"I know that. And I tried to explain to my naive younger self, but she wouldn't listen. She's determined to bring down that hub."

"She will fail."

"Yes. But she has weapons that I brought from the future. I believe you're familiar with them."

"Transphasic torpedoes. We will adapt."

"Eventually," the admiral agreed, "but not before *Voyager* does a great deal of damage." She paused, letting all this sink in, using her skill at dramatic timing to draw the Queen into her plan. "I'm willing to tell you how to adapt to those weapons *now.*"

Intrigued, the Queen began to enjoy the game. "In exchange for what?"

"I want you to send a cube to tractor *Voyager* . . . to drag them back to the Alpha Quadrant."

The Queen's metallic eyes narrowed. A creature who could not be manipulated? Says who?

After ten years of conniving and plotting and bargaining, the reaction gave Admiral Janeway monumental satisfaction. "They're going home whether they like it or not."

"You're asking me to believe that the incorruptible Kathryn Janeway," the Borg Queen plumbed, "would betray her own crew."

"Not betray them," the admiral countered. "Save them from themselves. I brought technology to help *Voyager* get home, but the captain's arrogant, self-righteous . . . and her officers are so blinded by loyalty that they're prepared to sacrifice their lives just to deal a crippling blow to the Borg."

The Queen raised her chin and said, "But *you'd* never try to harm us."

"I've become a pragmatist in my old age. All I want is to get that crew back to their families."

"You wish," the Queen added, "to insure the well-being of your 'collective.' I can appreciate that. I'll help you, Admiral . . . but it'll cost more than you're offering."

"What else do you want?"

"Your vessel and its database."

"I told you . . . I'll show you how to adapt their torpedoes—"

"Insufficient."

Admiral Janeway felt her plan begin to unravel. If the future were compromised—she was already tampering with repercussions out of sight, out of control. "If I let you assimilate technology from the future, there's no telling how events would be altered."

"You're willing to alter the future," the Queen pointed out, "by getting *Voyager* home now."

"Yes, but there's a difference."

Couldn't the Queen understand the difference? The admiral wanted to alter the future *her* way. She knew best. She knew what was going to happen if nothing changed. Why didn't everyone just take her word for what was the better course?

"Do what all good 'pragmatists' do, Admiral," the Queen challenged. "Compromise."

"All right, I'll give you the shuttle. *After* the ship arrives safely in the Alpha Quadrant."

The Queen smiled. "You've already lied to your younger self. How do I know you're not lying to me?"

"I guess you'll just have to trust me."

"That won't be necessary."

Was the Queen communicating with the Collective? She seemed suddenly more smug.

Admiral Janeway controlled her own expression. She had already given too much away.

"You've underestimated me, Admiral," the Queen said. "While we've been talking, my drones have triangulated on your signal—"

"Computer, deactivate interface! Deploy armor!"

Instantly she was back in her shuttle. The mental image of the Queen dissolved in less than a second. Was it too late? Was it?

The shuttle rocked from side to side. The cloak!

A beam had hold of her, forcing the shuttle to drop its cloaking energy!

Her arms and legs tensed. She felt the buzz of a Borg transporter beam. She'd been found!

CHAPTER 17

THE ADMIRAL MATERIALIZED IN FRONT OF THE BORG QUEEN—THIS time in the flesh—burdened with the knowledge that she had greatly miscalculated almost everything. She counted on the idea that the past was primitive and she had all the advantages. She had enjoyed her communication with the Queen, had taken time to enjoy herself after so many years of anticipation.

Now she was caught, and the Queen had her in the Unicomplex, and had possession of the shuttle without having had to come up to the admiral's deal.

This was a critical error, and Admiral Janeway had allowed it to happen.

"Very clever," the Borg Queen murmured, "hiding right on my doorstep. Were you planning to attack us from inside the Unicomplex?"

The admiral stiffened her lips. She must not speak, not give away anything more.

"Not feeling talkative?" the Queen chided. "That's all right."

The attack came again from the Queen's wrist, but this

time there was no protection from the technological shield of illusion. This time the admiral was physically here. The assimilation tubule hurt—a piercing agony at the admiral's throat. Borg technology began instantly to ripple beneath her skin.

"You and I don't need words to understand each other," the Queen said.

The admiral felt her body collapse, her eyes go dark. She gave herself to the the whispering web of a billion Borg voices on their way into her mind.

But she saw other things in her mind too. Now linked to the Collective, she also saw the the *Starship Voyager* plunge into the nebula clearing, back into the eye of threat's private hurricane. The bridge must be a tense place right now, alight with anxiety and excitement. And yet there was a thrill in the eyes of the officers, all of them as a team, with a single purpose—Janeway, Chakotay, Seven, Paris, Kim, Tuvok—all together again, strong and young. Despite the horrors, this was what they had all been trained for, what they had all intended to do with their talents when they signed on with Starfleet.

The transwarp hub loomed before the suddenly tiny ship. Without altering course or engaging evasive cautionary maneuvers, the ship entered one of the glowing apertures in the great wheel. With a flash of light, it disappeared.

The admiral had no idea whose point of view she was witnessing. She listened, helpless to move or react, to the voice of the Collective.

VOYAGER HAS ENTERED APERTURE EIGHT TWO THREE
ACCESS: TRANSWARP CORRIDOR ZERO NINE

* * *

ENDGAME

She now saw a mental picture of herself slumped against a console, her skin gray-blue, mottled, with Borg implants pressed to her features. Before her, the Borg Queen seemed satisfied and curious.

REDIRECT VESSELS TO INTERCEPT CORRIDOR NINE VOYAGER
U.S.S.

ZERO NINE TRANSWARP

INTERCEPT COMPLY JANEWAY JANEWAY

UNABLE TO COMPLY

The voices were suddenly muddled by a high-pitched whine. The Queen reacted with pain and stumbled.

Admiral Janeway summoned her sheer force of will and blinked her eyes. The whine began to die down, but the voices of the Borg cacophony were now poisoned with echoes and overlays, jumbled and disparate. There was a nonsensical ring to them now.

ZERO TRANSWARP

UNABLE

COMPLYING VOYAGER NINE CORRIDOR

The Queen spread her arms in disorientation. Panic painted itself across her face.

The admiral felt a tiny smile on her own lips. "Must be . . . something . . . you assimilated . . ."

"What have you done?" the Queen cried.

"I thought we didn't . . . need words to . . . understand each other."

The Queen endured a shooting pain. Beside her, a console exploded, bathing her in sparks. "You've infected us! A neurolytic pathogen!"

Admiral Janeway found the next smile much easier.

"Just enough to bring chaos to order," she said. Her voice was stronger! "Your conduit's shielding is destabilizing . . . look . . . let's watch together, Your Majesty . . . *Voyager* is firing its transphasic torpedoes . . . they're ripping through the interspatial manifold . . ."

"*Voyager* will be destroyed," the Queen spoke sluggishly.

"They're ahead of the shock waves," the admiral said, just to prove she knew. "They'll survive . . . Captain Janeway and I made sure of that . . . it's you who underestimated *us*."

Like bullets from a machine gun, transphasic torpedoes punched through the Borg hardware and kept delivering destruction on a long powerful trajectory. Violence erupted through the Queen's consoles. Sparks rained around them from destructive collapse high in the Unicomplex. The cry of a billion confused Borg blew through their minds like wind.

The transwarp hub, in all its gargantuan lordliness, began to collapse on itself as if dragged into a huge gravity well.

Near the admiral, the Queen's mechanical body jolted and convulsed in weird microcosmic empathy with her planet-sized counterparts. Her shoulder sparked. Like a piece of a store-bought plastic doll, her arm blew off and fell to the floor, leaving nothing but a nasty tendril dangling from the socket that once had fed her circuitry.

She didn't react to her arm's little dance, but instead the

Queen tilted her head and brought in a floating screen with a picture of a Borg sphere.

"Sphere six three four, they can still hear my thoughts."

She focused on the image, then closed her eyes and strained to send a telepathic command.

The admiral, nearly helpess in her half-Borg state, watched with a churning delight at the Queen's trouble. A disease, a plague, a virus—something so basic that it couldn't be out-thought.

Lovely.

Around them the entire complex began to shudder and spark, beautiful in its horror of destruction. Some things really were gorgeous as they blew themselves to molecules . . . suns, clouds, storms, Borg cubes . . .

Admiral Janeway indulged in her final moments by completely enjoying her long-planned revenge on the Borg, their "unbeatable" Queen, and their plans to assimilate the galaxy like a disease. Now they had the disease.

A shot of pain racked the Queen's body again and in an almost burlesque sideshow way one of her legs fell off. She grabbed a console to steady herself and glared at the admiral.

"Captain Janeway is about to die," she threatened. "If she has no future . . . you'll never exist . . . and nothing you've done here today will happen."

But there was pleasure in possibility. The admiral noted that the Queen's voice was losing its aural stability. As explosions tore through the complex around them, the Queen's body pulled itself to pieces like the finishing sequence of some kind of Frankenstein story.

In the admiral's assimilated mind, still clinging by virtue of the virus to a tincture of humanity, she enjoyed the invigorating sight of Borg cubes, Borg spheres, and the transwarp hub being chewed by crawling brushfire all through the systems. Drones scrambled everywhere, helpless, in their brainless effort to continue doing their jobs. They didn't know they were about to die. Insects stumbling everywhere, still tending the nest while the grass burned around them. How ironic!

There were disadvantages to linking every being, every circuit and brain cell, every eye and voice being linked inextricably. To the glories of the swarm would come a unified death. Admiral Janeway was glad to share their end with them. Rather than waste away in an unhappy future, she would have a hero's finish while doing heroic things. Her crew would live now, and the Borg would suffer damage possibly irreparable.

Their ambitious Queen was dissolving before her eyes. The Collective was being consumed in a giant meltdown.

And I did it. I always knew I would.

"Full power. Continue firing. Take out as much as you can! Concentrate on the connective junctions! Seven, show them their targets!"

"I'm having trouble holding course," Paris warned as the ship bucked to starboard and whined in an attempt to compensate. "Permission to transfer power to specified thrusters."

"Do what you have to," Janeway said. "Don't wait for orders. Keep us on a heading to the Alpha Quadrant."

"That's my point—it keeps changing!"

"Seven, help him! Identify and shut down the systems that are confusing the helm."

"Aye, Captain."

"Aft armor is down to six percent," Tuvok called.

Kim spoke at almost the same time. "Hull breaches on decks seven through twelve!"

"Evacuate those decks. Shut down all unnecessary systems. Tell the crew to batten down and hang on!"

Paris was sweating by the pint. "I can't stay ahead of them, Captain!"

The ship endured a hard bang.

"The armor is failing," Tuvok reported.

Chakotay grabbed the rail and called to Seven, "Where's the nearest aperture?"

"Approximately thirty seconds ahead—but it leads back to the Delta Quadrant!"

Chakotay turned to the captain. It was the easy way out, the quick way to save themselves.

Janeway endured his gaze. Save the ship? Or keep taking the only chance they had for a quick way home?

No—no more safety-first!

"Mr. Paris, prepare to adjust your heading!"

"The helm's sluggish—"

"Draw whatever power you need. Compromise life-support if you have to. We can't breathe if we're all dead anyway!"

"Yes, ma'am!"

The ship veered hard over, bending to port and several degrees down.

"Seven, give us a course!" Janeway called. "The nearest aperture to the Alpha Quadrant!"

"We'll have to loop full about again, Captain," she reported instantly. "Six-six mark six."

"You're kidding . . ."

"Six-six mark six!"

"Mr. Paris, you have your numbers. Effect change of course! Tuvok, keep firing the torpedoes down to the last salvo! Let's drag down as much of the Borg idea of life while we have the chance."

"Captain, what about the admiral?" Chakotay asked, calling above the whine and splatter of electrical breakouts around the bridge. "Aren't you going to tell me?" He moved a little closer, holding himself near her in spite of the shaking. "She's not theoretical, you know . . . she's a living person here."

"A person who made her own choice about when and where to give up her life. She's fulfilling her own dream," Janeway said thoughtfully. "You're not going to suggest I don't know what she's thinking, are you?"

"No." Chakotay wiped the sweat off his face. "Not at all, Kathryn. I think we both know her pretty well. I just don't like leaving her," he added, cupping her hand with his, "even though I'm bringing her with me."

Janeway stole a moment from the violence and battle to meet his eyes and touch his hand. "Don't worry, old friend. If we get through, the admiral and I have a rendezvous with a whole new destiny. We all will."

Chakotay, usually unflappable and wry in his dealings even with the ghastly or unpredicted, endured a little shudder of childlike anticipation that Janeway felt all the way down his arm and into her hand. Were they really going home? Was this really it after seven years of wandering? Or would one great salvo from the Borg cut them off at the last kilometer?

No. Captain Janeway willed the universe to go her way this time, this one final time!

"Captain, a Borg sphere is bearing down on our stern," Tuvok warned quickly.

The sphere immediately opened up on the ship, chewing away at the armor around the nacelles and engineering hull and the aft end of the saucer section.

Tuvok frowned. "Armor is eroding steadily!"

"Increase speed," Janeway ordered.

"Captain!"

Janeway looked up at Tom Paris's warning cry at the main screen. Before them the corridor between quadrants was collapsing in on itself!

CHAPTER 18

Pathfinder Research Lab
Stardate 54989.1

REG BARCLAY WAS ALL RIGHT WHILE HE WAS BY HIMSELF. HE could concentrate on the wild readings pulsing through the equipment and the numbers, waves, and sensory data pouring like water through the arrays. Borg information.

The whole base was at red alert. Ten admirals were on their way. Within minutes of his report, the doors opened and dozens of Starfleet personnel scrambled to the lab areas that had previously been pretty much Barclay's lonely domain. He now had more help than anybody would ever want.

When Admiral Paris arrived with Admirals Barrenson, Eddu, Sylvanus, and two others whom Barclay didn't know, he suddenly found himself at the hub of the next great thing to happen in Federation history.

Or the end of the Federation once and for all. Nobody was forgetting that part, were they?

"Mr. Barclay, what is it you think you've got here?" Admiral Paris asked quickly. "Tell me in your own words."

"A transwarp aperture," Barclay stammered. "It's less than a light-year from Earth!"

"How many Borg vessels?"

"We can't get a clear reading. But the graviton emissions are off the scale!"

"I want every ship in range to converge on those coordinates."

The other admirals broke immediately to summon whichever ships of their own fleets were within range of communications.

Admiral Sylvanus came back within thirty seconds and said, "We've got eighteen ships forming into position. Nine more on the way."

And those were only the ones in the solar system. Within an hour there would be thirty more, Barclay guessed, rushing here at high warp. They would either be battling Borg or be the cleanup crew.

On the big screen the aperture glowed like the mouth of hell itself. Between the base and the aperture, eighteen Starfleet ships of various configuration converged and maneuvered into formation. Barclay shivered down a sense of the impending— that was a lot of firepower concentrated on one little area, but would it be enough?

"Open a channel," Admiral Paris ordered.

Barclay almost forgot the admiral was talking to him. He snapped out of his fascination with the screen's alarming tale and pounded the comm panel, then nodded to the admiral.

"This is Admiral Paris. Use all necessary force. I repeat—all necessary force."

One by one acknowledgments shot through the system from each of the Starfleet ships. They were still jockeying for position. It had to be right, or they could accidently graze each other. Was it right? Were they in a good position? Or would accidents happen?

Barclay's heart pounded in his ears. His eyes were nearly blinded by the brightness of the opening aperture, so much that when he looked down at his controls he couldn't read them. He shook his head, rubbed his eyes, and fought to see. With one hand he shielded the controls until the readings began to appear in the cloud before him.

"Sir, there's a vessel coming through!"

"Identify!"

"Borg signature!"

"This is Admiral Paris. All ships confirm visual of Borg infiltration. Target and open fire!"

Smart, Barclay noticed. Even if the equipment said Borg, the admiral and all those captains wanted to be sure of what they were shooting at.

Barclay forgot about his console and looked up into the viewscreen. The bright light of the aperture framed a corona around a dark shadowy ball, as if a solar eclipse had come right up to give Earth a kiss. An instant later and the sphere began to define itself, showing hard edges and square shadows, rectangular depressions and mechanicals formations and portals.

A Borg sphere! Visual confirmation!

The Starfleet ships opened fire in a bright ballet. The sphere's shields flashed, creating a ghostly blue bubble around the sphere as if the ball were inside blown glass.

"Phaser fire is not breaching their shields, sir," Barclay responded. "We can't fight them with conventional weapons!"

"We can sure as hell try. All ships, reconfigure and continue firing. Deploy photon torpedoes, tandem salvos."

The admiral's voice got steadier as the situation grew more dire. That was the sign of a leader!

Barclay looked at the admiral, just to record this moment in his mind.

When he looked back to his controls and the viewscreen, he pointed at the aperture behind the flashing Borg sphere and the ships firing wildly upon it. "Admiral, another formation! Another ship!"

More Borg!

They couldn't fight *more* Borg. The other Starfleet ships would never get here in time. This was a full-fledged invasion from the Delta Quadrant!

Barclay almost swallowed his whole head. Good thing he wasn't giving the orders, because he could barely speak.

"Federation-wide Mayday," Admiral Paris croaked. "Broadcast emergency alert to every planet. All planetary defenses should prepare for aggressive—"

"Sir!" Barclay pointed at the screen.

A streaking body emerged from within the aperture, but not a ship—a single thin line of propulsive trail. The streak lit into the sphere and drilled deep.

Barclay wanted to glance at the admiral, to measure the other man's expression and see what he should be thinking, but he couldn't pull his eyes away. They didn't know what they were seeing. The Starfleet armada hadn't had that effect—even if their phasers could have produced such destruction, they weren't firing from inside the aperture.

From far within the bowels of the sphere, an explosion began. The whole sphere engaged in a great burp from inside, ejecting plumes of orange plasma and superheated gas. The sphere's hardware skin became a sheath housing a fireball. A moment later, that fireball blew outward.

All the other admirals began to cluster behind Admiral Paris and Barclay. For this moment they were only confused spectators of a monumental performance, the utter wrecking of a Borg sphere. They couldn't decide how to act or which orders to give until they had some idea of what they were seeing. They stood shoulder to shoulder, witnesses to the next unbelievable moment—when the Borg sphere disengaged its central adhesion and broke apart into an encompassing fireball.

The blazing eruption blew outward in all directions, bathing the Starfleet ships in white-hot ejecta. If the crews on those bridges weren't cheering, they weren't watching.

In a phenomenal breach of—well, everything—Barclay reached out and seized the admiral's arm. "Sir, sir! Look!"

Ridiculous—the admiral was already looking, but Barclay was drowning in sheer thrill.

"Oh, sir!" he cried like a kid at a baseball game.

The green-white-golden fireball broke up as a solid form punched through at dead center. A recognizable shape—a Starfleet shape!

"Cease fire!" Admiral Paris called. "All ships, cease fire! We have Starfleet contact! My God!"

The senior officer dropped his demeanor of stability and gasped at what they saw. Some of the other admirals reached over to pat Admiral Paris on his back and shoulders.

"Voyager!" Barclay choked out. "It's *Voyager!"*

A cheer broke from the admirals around him, as simple and childlike as he could ever imagine, and the sound thrilled him to his core.

ENDGAME

The admiral gazed at his son's ship as it soared forward through the veil of glorious debris and streaked toward the Starfleet armada.

Beside him, Reg Barclay quietly spoke the words all were thinking.

"They're home . . ."

Admiral Paris held his breath for a moment of communion with this miracle, then found his voice.

"Hail them, please, Mr. Barclay."

"My pleasure, sir! Where's the comm—oh! Short-range! Imagine that! This is . . . this is . . . Pathfinder Base to *Voyager.* Come in!"

CHAPTER 19

THE CHEERING ON *VOYAGER*'S BRIDGE WAS A BALM FOR THE SOUL. Kathryn Janeway sank back into her chair and waved away their moment of joy. There would be time for celebrating later, and plenty of cheering. Why, Starfleet might even bring back the ticker-tape parade.

Home . . . home. All of them, healthy and together.

When Admiral Paris's face, flanked by Reg Barclay and several other admirals, appeared on the main screen, Janeway almost laughed. They were perfectly stunned. Imagine rocking a fistful of admirals into silence!

"Janeway to Pathfinder Base. Sorry to surprise you . . . next time we'll call ahead."

Admiral Paris smiled shakily. "Welcome back, Captain."

"It's good to be here."

"How did you—"

"It'll all be in my report, sir."

"I'll look forward to it!"

He didn't ask how his son was doing, or any other questions. Maybe he was afraid to know.

Tom Paris gazed at the vision of his father. He was hardly the rash young pilot who had disappeared off the scopes seven years ago, and had made his peace with the man whose face was their first beacon back to the Alpha Quadrant.

The admiral clicked off the communications connection. Probably unable to speak right now, as were most of them. Around her, her crew gazed at the armada of welcoming ships on the screen and the beautiful marbleized ball of Earth in the near distance. Seven and Chakotay were looking at each other now. Paris was still gazing at the screen and its wonders. Tuvok glanced at Janeway, and she was gratified to see him so healthy. Harry Kim was almost in tears with sheer joy, and choked into silence.

Around them, the sounds of damage reports and scramblings around the ship were wonderful music. In minutes they would have help, real help. They could call in the experts who had built this ship. There would be parts galore. Energy and resources and expertise brimming from every crack. For the first time, there would be plenty of everything, and the next time Janeway hailed her crew on the shipwide, she would be imparting to them the wonderful news. They could be home for supper.

"Sickbay to Lieutenant Paris."

Everybody flinched. The call was so mundane, so common— yet they all knew what it meant.

Paris almost fell out of his chair when the doctor's voice was backdropped by an infant's thready wail.

"There's someone here who'd like to say hello."

Paris whirled around in his chair. Janeway smiled at him.

"You'd better get down there, Tom," she invited. "Mr. Chakotay, take the helm."

"Aye, Captain!" Chakotay snapped.

He slid into the chair as Tom Paris dodged for the lift, catching the hands of his shipmates as he rushed past.

Captain Janeway squared herself in her chair and assessed her victories. The Borg transwarp network had imploded. The way to the Delta Quadrant was sealed up, and the ship and its crew were finally home. Her mission was complete. She had delivered the starship to its rightful owners, and her crewmates to their families and futures.

She settled back and murmured, "Thanks for everything, Admiral Janeway . . ."

Chakotay alone heard her, or heard something. He turned. "Course, Captain?"

She turned and gave him an ironic smile. Then she gave an order she had given many times over the last seven years.

"Set a course for home," she said firmly.

Home.

STAR TREK VOYAGER®
HOMECOMING

Christie Golden

**Coming Summer 2003
in Mass Market
from Pocket Books**

Now the laborer's task is o'er;
Now the battle day is past;
Now upon the farther shore
Lands the voyager at last.

CHAPTER 1

TOM PARIS LOOKED AT THE NEWBORN, ONLY A FEW MINUTES OLD, cradled awkwardly in his arms. She weighed only a few kilos, but felt so solid, so real to him. Her skin was reddish brown and wrinkled. Thick, coarse black hair covered her skull, larger even than a human baby's. Small ridges furrowed her brow, which he traced with a tender finger. As he watched, she yawned and waved a tiny fist in the air, almost defiantly, as if she dared anyone to come between her and a nap.

"She's the most beautiful thing I've ever seen," he said, and even as he acknowledged his daughter's wrinkled ugliness, he knew the words were completely true. He glanced over at B'Elanna. "Except, of course, for her mother."

Gently, he sat down on the sickbay bed beside her as she smiled tiredly at him. "Nice save," she said, with a hint of her old robust demeanor.

"How's Mommy feeling?" he asked.

"Mommy's felt better," she admitted, and extended her arms for the child.

"Mother and child are just fine, though Mother is understandably cranky," said the Doctor. "You should be able to return to duty in approximately three days, Lieutenant. I feel compelled to inform you that I have downloaded everything in the database on the care of both Klingon and human infants." He preened a bit. "I'd make an excellent baby-sitter."

Tom grinned and gave his wife the baby, and his arms felt oddly empty as B'Elanna guided the child to her breast. He could get into this whole father thing, he thought.

"Janeway to Lieutenant Paris."

Tom grimaced, then replied, "Paris here."

"Report to my ready room."

He looked at B'Elanna. "Aye, Captain." Reluctantly he rose. "I thought we were on parental leave, but apparently duty calls. Sorry, girls."

B'Elanna gave him a strange expression that he couldn't read. She reached out and touched his face tenderly. "I love you, Tom."

Now, why would she pick this time to say that? What was going on in that head of hers? "I love you too," he said, taking the hand that caressed his cheek and kissing it. "Both of you. Be back as soon as I can."

When he reached the bridge, he was surprised to see Captain Janeway sitting in her command chair, not in the ready room. He raised an eyebrow in question. In response, she nodded toward the room. "In the ready room, Mr. Paris."

This was getting downright confusing. "Yes ma'am," he said.

The door hissed open. An imposing-looking, white-haired man rose from where he had been sitting at Janeway's desk. Tom's throat went dry.

"Dad," he breathed. Then, snapping to attention, he said, "Your pardon, sir. I mean, good day, Admiral Paris."

Of course this was going to happen. Admiral Owen Paris had been heavily involved in Project *Voyager.* Tom knew that. Of course, as the project's nominal head, Paris would be the first to board the lost vessel finally returned home. But Tom had been so thoroughly engrossed in thoughts of his wife and child that the likelihood that he would soon be reunited with his father had completely skipped his mind. Now he understood B'Elanna's peculiar look as he had left. Even she had figured it out before he had.

Admiral Paris's face was carefully neutral. *Damn,* thought Tom, *he looks so much older, so much more careworn.* The seven years that had passed since they last spoke had not been kind to him. Tom wondered how he appeared in his father's eyes.

Admiral Paris folded his hands behind his back, echoing his son's formal stance.

"Lieutenant Paris. It's . . . it's good to see you. I'm glad you completed your mission so successfully. Your captain has many glowing things to say about you."

"No more than I have to say about her, sir. It's been a privilege to serve with her these past seven years." Why were his eyes stinging so? And that lump in his throat . . .

Later, Tom would never be able to remember just which of them had made the first move. Maybe both of them did. But the next thing he knew, he was in his father's arms. It was a sensation he had not experienced since—he couldn't remember. Had his father ever embraced him so freely, so tightly, before? Had *he* ever wanted to open his arms to the rigid authority figure the untouchable, aloof Admiral Paris had always represented?

It didn't matter. His head resting on his father's shoulder, Tom smelled the familiar scent of aftershave, and for the first time, really believed that, finally, he was going home.

"Dad," he whispered, brokenly.

"My boy," Owen Paris replied, his own voice hoarse. "My boy. I'm so glad you're home."

They sat and talked for a long, long time. Paris noted that they avoided anything of real import, like whether or not he'd be put back in jail or the fact that Admiral Paris was a grandfather. Tom was shocked to learn that, on a whim, his father had decided to take a cooking class and was laughing out loud at an anecdote about what "blackened chicken" *really* meant when the door hissed open.

Janeway stood there, smiling. "I wanted to give you some time alone together before I called the senior staff for Admiral Paris's preliminary debriefing. Tom, does he know . . . ?" She lifted an eyebrow in question.

"Before we begin, Captain," said Tom, standing straight with pride, "is there time for my father to meet his daughter-in-law and granddaughter?"

Admiral Paris came as close to openmouthed gaping as Tom had ever seen in his life. Tension raced through him. Time to drop the other shoe: "B'Elanna will be so happy to see you, sir."

He knew Admiral Paris knew who B'Elanna Torres was. A half-Klingon, and, like his son, a former Maquis. Silently, Tom pleaded that the fragile new camaraderie they had just established would weather this new storm.

There was a long, taut pause. Then a slow smile spread across the lined face. "It would be a pleasure."

When Tuvok reported to sickbay per the Doctor's orders, he felt a rush of surprise, which he quelled at once. Standing there calmly, his hands folded behind his back, was his eldest son, Sek.

"Greetings, Father," said Sek calmly. "It is good to see you."

"And you, my son. I assume that the Doctor requested your presence to administer the *fal-tor-voh?*"

Sek nodded. "Admiral Paris contacted me approximately fourteen hours ago. I studied the disease extensively during my voyage to rendezvous with *Voyager.* I believe I am adequately prepared to meld with you, Father."

Privately, Tuvok wondered. A few hours spent reading material on such an intricate, complicated procedure hardly rendered his son, intelligent though he was, "adequately prepared." But he knew the situation was worsening. He looked over at the Doctor, who answered Tuvok's wordless question.

"The genetic link is more important than actual familiarity with the procedure," the Doctor said. "And frankly, Commander, time is of the essence. I don't think anything would be served by waiting until Sek has learned more."

"Very well," said Tuvok. To Sek, he said, "We'll return to my quarters."

"If you don't mind," said the Doctor, "I'd rather have you here, so I can monitor your response. Not to insult you, Sek, but there's a chance that something might go wrong."

"It is impossible to insult me, Doctor," Sek replied. "I have no emotional response to critiques or commentary on my skills or lack thereof. Therefore, I can neither be flattered nor insulted."

"Vulcans," the Doctor muttered, rolling his eyes. Tuvok hesitated. This was an intimate, private ceremony. And yet, he was forced to admit that the Doctor had logic on his side. Reluctantly, he lay down on the biobed. He glanced over to see B'Elanna watching him; then she quickly looked away and returned her attention to nursing her child.

"I offer my congratulations on the healthy birth of your child," he said, somewhat stiffly.

"Thank you, Tuvok," she replied. She offered no question or commentary on what she was witnessing, for which Tuvok was silently grateful. "Doctor," she said suddenly, "Tom and his father are coming down to meet me and Miral. I'd like to receive them in my quarters, if that's all right."

"As long as you go directly from that bed to your bed, you should be fine. The brief walk won't hurt you, and actually would be good for you. But if you start feeling weak, let me know at once, and don't overtire yourself."

"Believe me, I won't," said Torres. She eased out of bed, tapped her combadge, and, cradling the infant, headed out of sickbay while talking. "Tom, can you meet us in our quarters? I'm getting very tired of sickbay. . . ."

Tuvok gazed after her, thankful for her discretion. The Doctor brought a chair for Sek, then placed cortical monitors on both Vulcans' heads. Discreetly, he stepped as far away as possible.

Tuvok looked up at his son. To his consternation, he felt a rush of emotion. He had missed his family so much. Sek saw the reaction and recognized it for what it was: a sign that the disease was progressing.

"Do not worry, Father," he said gently. "Soon, these distractions will be gone." Sek closed his eyes, calming himself, then reached and placed his long, slim fingers on his father's brow. "My mind to your mind . . . your thoughts to my thoughts . . ."

Sek's presence in his mind was like oil poured on churning water to Tuvok. At first, there was only a surface calm; then, gradually, Sek's thoughts penetrated deeper. He felt the young man's mind traversing his own, finding and searching out the synapses that carried the destructive virus.

He and his son had not melded since Sek was an infant. Tuvok, T'Pel, and Sek had bonded then in an extremely deep and profound union of minds. It was an ancient rite that dated back to when Vulcans first began to harness the incredible powers of the mind. It had been easiest to meld with family members with whom one shared blood, then with more distant relatives, then strangers and, finally in recent history, members of other species. But the initial bonding, established so that the helpless infant could be linked to his parents more firmly, had always been sacred and powerful.

It was this familiarity that swept through Tuvok now. The irony was not lost on him that this time, it was his son who was nurturing him, not the other way around. The bonding was to protect father, not child.

Sek's thoughts raced through Tuvok's mind, finding the damaged part of the older Vulcan's brain. There they were, the mutated cells, and Tuvok could see in his mind's eye that they were unnatural and out of harmony with the complex, delicate balance that was the Vulcan brain. The disease was spread through the neurological pathways. Tuvok knew that Sek, whose mind was undamaged, would be instructing his father's own cells to protect the uninfected part of the brain. The blood bond between them magnified the intimacy of the connection. It was the only way the condition could have been treated. Reaching so deeply would not have been possible without that link.

On a cellular level, Sek began to "speak" to Tuvok's brain. *There has been damage here. These cells are dangerous. You are not to access them any longer.* Gently, but firmly, Sek urged the cells to put up their own barriers. Information and stimuli were henceforth to bypass these areas. They were to become inert. Tuvok felt a strange rush, an imaginary tingling sensation as, under Sek's gentle urging, areas of his brain that had hitherto never been used opened up and responded to stimuli. Cell by cell, Sek isolated and rerouted the way Tuvok's brain would function. For several long minutes, Sek gently disentangled his own thoughts from Tuvok's.

Just before Sek withdrew, Tuvok felt a powerful, joyful wave wash through him. It was the love that his son felt for his father, the delight at being able to help him. Tuvok saw a small Vulcan child, and knew it to be his granddaughter T'meni, named for Tuvok's own mother. They would not speak of it, but here, in the most intimate joining that was possible for any two Vulcans, Tuvok accepted that love and returned it as passionately.

Then his thoughts were his alone. He opened his eyes and gazed up into the impassive visage of Sek.

"How do you feel?" asked the Doctor.

Tuvok sat up, looked from his son to the Doctor, and announced, "I believe am cured."

When the door hissed open, B'Elanna tried hard not to look as worried and apprehensive as she felt. Tom had told her only that he and Admiral Paris were coming down to meet her and Miral. He had told her nothing of how their own meeting went. She had guessed it had gone well because of the lightness in her husband's voice, but it could have been an act for overhearing ears.

But when she saw Tom's nearly ear-to-ear grin—the grin she saw only when he was so happy he simply could not wipe it from his face, no matter how hard he tried to play cool and collected—she knew that her worries had been for nothing.

And when the imposing Admiral Owen Paris, practically a legend in his own time, reached toward her with outstretched hands, clasped her own, and kissed her warmly on the cheek, she almost wept.

"My son always had an eye for beauty," said Admiral Paris. "I'm pleased to see that he has learned to value character as well. I've read your captain's report on you, Lieu—B'Elanna. Both of you seem to have won her respect and affections."

"Thank you, Admiral," she said, her voice thick.

"You may call me Owen, if you like," he said. "Now, let me see this lovely little grandchild of mine."

Torres handed Miral over to her grandfather and reached for Tom's hand. The older man handled the tiny infant with surprising grace, smiling down into her little face with obvious pleasure.

"You handle babies quite well . . . Owen," said Torres, trying out the name with caution.

Admiral Paris smiled. "I've spent enough time with them. You never knew, Tom, that I was the one in charge of diaper changing, did you?"

Judging by Tom's dumbfounded expression, he clearly did not. Torres smothered a smile at the thought of this distinguished elderly man changing Tom's soiled diapers, but the ease with which he carried Miral made his statement believable. He looked down at his new daughter-in-law and the smile faded somewhat.

"Tom and I discussed your family situation on our way here," he said. B'Elanna felt the heat of embarrassment rise in her cheeks. "I understand that you are without family."

"Not entirely correct," she said. "My father . . . chose not to be with me and my mother many years ago. I spoke to him for the first time in years just weeks ago. I have reason to believe that my mother died while we were in the Delta Quadrant."

"That was what Tom said," Admiral Paris confirmed. "I wanted to tell you that now, you do have family. Close family. You and Miral are now dear and valued members of the Paris clan. My wife and I will love you like our own child." He turned to look at Tom and said, "And that is a great deal indeed."

Torres smiled, even though she felt like crying with joy. "Thank you, sir. That means a lot to us."

"Now, when *Voyager* first appeared," Admiral Paris continued, "we of course immediately notified all families. Nearly everyone has recorded messages from loved ones. Once I learned who my new daughter-in-law was, I checked to see if we had any for her. We did—two."

Torres's breath caught. She couldn't think of any one person who'd want to send her a message, let alone two. Admiral Paris handed them to her. "If you'd like to view them in private, Tom and I can—"

"No." B'Elanna spoke swiftly. "You are my family now. Whatever this is, whoever sent it, you can watch it with me."

After a moment, Tom nodded, and activated the viewscreen.

A handsome man with Torres's dark hair and eyes appeared. B'Elanna stared, disbelieving.

Father.

"Hello, again, B'Elanna," he said softly. "You said you would write, but I know you've been busy. I want you to know that I'm so glad you're coming safely home." He hesitated. "I have a lot of explaining to do. I hope you'll let me do it. I want so badly to see you again, to try to put things right . . . if they can be put right. If you've decided you don't want to see me, I'll understand. But I want to let you know that I love you, and that I'm sorry. Maybe you're old enough to understand that, and forgive me. I won't come to the banquet if you don't want me to. I'll wait to hear from you. If I don't . . . well, that's my answer."

He blinked rapidly and his eyes looked very bright. "I love you, my little one. I hope to see you soon."

She felt Tom's arm around her, felt Admiral Paris's sympathetic gaze. She swallowed hard.

"Do you want to see him?" Tom asked, very softly.

"I—I don't know," she managed. She fumbled for the second message and handed it to Tom. "Let's see who this one's from."

Tom inserted the disk. A lovely but stern Klingon visage appeared, one Torres didn't recognize, and said, "I am Commander Logt. We must soon meet and speak of your mother. It is a matter of some urgency."

Torres recalled the words her mother had spoken in Grethor, the Klingon hell:

We will see each other again.

In Sto-Vo-Kor.

In Sto-Vo-Kor . . . or maybe . . . when you get home.

Perhaps this Logt knew what her mother had meant.

Janeway's heart lifted as Tuvok entered the room. Their eyes met, and he nodded. That was all she was going to get out of him, but it was enough. The *fal-tor-voh* had been successful. He would require regular, mild doses of medication to keep the disease from recurring, but the dreadful mental deterioration of which her future self had warned had been averted. How easily it had been accomplished; how devastating it would have been to watch this beloved friend fall to pieces slowly, irreversibly, in front of her eyes.

She permitted herself the briefest pang of envy. Both Paris and Tuvok had already gotten to see family members, and they had been in the Alpha Quadrant for only a few hours. Of course, their situations had been unique. Paris's father had been the head of this project and had been involved on a professional as well as personal level. And getting Sek to his father had been a true emergency. They were traveling slowly on their way back to

Earth, in order to get all the necessary red tape cut before their arrival. And, she thought, not to overwhelm her crew. Certainly, they wanted to get home and see their loved ones. But the whole thing had happened so suddenly, so unexpectedly, that it had been quite a shock. One of the first things Janeway requested, besides Sek's presence, was a counselor. Her request had been granted as well as she could wish. The *Enterprise* had sent its own counselor, one Deanna Troi, who had also apparently been at least peripherally involved with Project *Voyager.* Upon greeting the dark-haired, soft-spoken woman, Janeway had immediately felt confident in her abilities. Her crew was fortunate to have this capable woman to turn to.

Tuvok slipped quietly into a seat and everyone turned his or her attention to Admiral Paris.

The admiral didn't immediately launch into his speech. He took a moment to look at each of them in turn, smiling a little. Janeway was pleased to see his eyes linger affectionately on his new daughter-in-law. Torres had insisted on being present despite doctor's orders, and the Doctor was keeping a close eye on her. Despite the slight risk, Janeway was glad she was here.

"There aren't words to articulate how happy I am to see you all here," Owen Paris began. "It's difficult to believe that in a few hours you'll be home. We've been sending you information for some time, so you know about the Dominion War and its outcome. But there are some questions many of you, especially the former Maquis among you, must still be concerned about.

"During the last days of the war there was a shortage of trained, capable officers. The situation was desperate. A general pardon was therefore offered to any of the Maquis who chose to return to Starfleet, absolving them of their betrayal and desertion, and after the massacre on Tevlik's moon, it was argued that there was no reason to doubt their commitment to the cause. To be honest, I opposed the amnesty. I did not think Maquis could be trusted. I have never been so happy to be proven wrong. The former Maquis served bravely and loyally. Therefore, I hereby extend the amnesty to all those who Captain Janeway informs me have served her so well."

Admiral Paris smiled, then spoke again. "Which means I am spared the unpleasant duty of escorting my new daughter-in-law to prison."

There were smiles all around. Come to think of it, mused Janeway, there had been a lot of smiles on this ship over the last several hours. She met Chakotay's eyes. They hadn't spoken of it—there was no point, he knew that she would have to surrender him to the authorities if it came to that—but Janeway felt a fierce surge of joy to know that he, along with every other member of the crew, would be returning home a hero, not a prisoner.

"But it won't be a utopia to which you'll be returning, either," Admiral Paris continued. "War is never easy, but this one has truly been a hell to endure. It's taken a terrible toll on everyone. We lost millions. We'll need all of you to pitch in and help us rebuild."

"You can count on us, Admiral," Janeway assured him.

"I'm sure I can," said the admiral. "After all, you should be well rested—you've had a pretty long break."

There was a general chuckle, and Janeway knew the admiral meant nothing negative by the remark. Nonetheless, it stung. This hadn't been a seven-year picnic. They'd been in some terrible battles. She'd lost good people, and had suffered her own private pains at the things she'd been forced to do . . . and forced not to do.

At the same time, in a way they had been lucky. Who knew who would have survived and who wouldn't have, had they all been in the Alpha Quadrant during the Dominion War? Maybe she'd have lost even more crewmen. But maybe they could have made a difference, too. Shortened the war, somehow.

She shook the thoughts off, both the good and the bad. The situation was what it was. They were about to come home, and, as the admiral had said, pitch in and help the Alpha Quadrant rebuild.

"And now," the admiral was saying, "there's someone else you need to meet."

The air beside him shimmered, and when the image solidified, Janeway saw the large-eyed, earnest Reginald Barclay. His face split into an enormous grin.

"Gosh," he said, "it's so good to finally get to see you all."

And regardless of what either Janeway or Admiral Paris had in mind, the room erupted into shouts and whoops as her well-trained, disciplined senior staff literally overturned chairs in order to embrace the man who had risked everything to bring them home.

CHAPTER 2

WHEN JANEWAY MATERIALIZED IN THE TRANSPORTER ROOM OF THE *Enterprise,* she was pleased and flattered but not altogether surprised to see that none other than Captain Jean-Luc Picard was present to greet her.

"Permission to come aboard," she said lightly.

"Very happily granted," he replied, stepping forward with his hand outstretched. Janeway grasped it and swiftly covered it with her other hand.

"Kathryn," he said heartily, his hazel eyes warm with affection. "My God, it's good to see you. I could scarcely believe it when I saw *Voyager* soaring toward us out of that cloud of debris," he said. "We had been ready to fight the Borg, not welcome home a lost traveler."

"What can I say?" she quipped. "I like to make an entrance."

"Now that, you certainly did," said Picard. He extended an arm, indicating that she should precede him. "We had hoped you'd make it home one of these days. We just never imagined it would be quite so soon."

She smiled as they walked down the corridor to the turbolift. This whole meeting with Picard had a resonance that he could not possibly understand. Perhaps one day she'd tell him about it.

"I understand Reginald Barclay served with you before being assigned to Project *Voyager*," she said. "I must congratulate you. We'd still be quite a long way away if not for his diligence."

"Hard to believe that he used to be our problem child, isn't it?" Picard replied. "Yes, he's done us all proud. We've got a few moments before the, ah, 'Inquisition' begins. Would you care to join me in my ready room for a cup of coffee?"

She was pleased that he remembered her fondness for the beverage. She was about to accept when she thought about someone else who had a great deal to do with the fact that *Voyager* had made it safely home. That someone had given her life for all of them, and at the very least, she deserved a toast with her favorite beverage.

"Do you know," Janeway said, "I think I'd like to share a pot of Earl Grey with you instead. I have a hunch that I'm going to learn to like tea."

The debriefing began at 1300. Picard, Captains Rixx and DeSoto, and Admirals Paris, Brackett, Montgomery, Amerman, and Berg were present. Janeway was reminded of having to give her orals back at the Academy. Thanks to Barclay, *Voyager* had been able to transmit ship's logs covering several years, so Starfleet had already accessed much of what her crew had learned in the Delta Quadrant. If it had not been for that, Janeway imagined her debriefing alone would have taken days. As it was, there were only a few perfunctory questions, and when Janeway tried to elaborate, Montgomery, the admiral in charge, cut her off curtly each time.

Admiral Kenneth Montgomery had a long, lean face with piercing gray eyes. With his thick, fair hair and muscular build, he could have been strikingly handsome, but there was an iciness about him that discouraged anything but the most professional, to-the-point interaction. She knew him by reputation only: he had been one of the key players in the war that had just recently ended. Janeway could see him easily in that role, and was grateful that Starfleet had had him.

But what did men like that do when there was peace?

More attention was given to *Voyager*'s interaction with the Borg. Even there, the questions were specific and Janeway was none too gently urged to reply with equal specificity. Montgomery leaned forward when she began to speak of the most recent battle. From time to time, Janeway could see his jaw tensing.

"Now," Montgomery said when she had done, "where did you acquire this latest technology with which *Voyager* is equipped?"

She smiled a little. "Well, it's actually Starfleet technology. You just haven't figured it out yet."

Montgomery glared at her. "An official debriefing with three captains and four admirals is no place for jokes, Captain Janeway."

Her eyes narrowed. "I assure you, Admiral, I fully appreciate the seriousness of this matter. I'm wondering if everyone here does. We seem to be racing through this debriefing when—"

"You say this is Starfleet technology, Captain," Montgomery interrupted. "Explain."

Choosing her words carefully to keep the explanation as brief as possible, Janeway explained about her future self returning to save *Voyager* and help them destroy the Borg transwarp hub. Montgomery's icy eyes flashed as she spoke and his jaw tightened, but he did not interrupt.

Janeway finished. There was a long, cold pause. Finally, Montgomery said in a flat voice, "Do you have any idea how many general orders you've violated, Captain?"

"Ken," said Paris gently, "first of all, she didn't do it. A twenty-six-years-older version of her did. And besides, you've got to admit there are extenuating circumstances." The admiral's words were delivered in a calm and mild fashion, but his face was hard. Montgomery seemed about to retort, then nodded.

"We'll send over some of our best people and begin analyzing this . . . this futuristic technology immediately. This hearing is over."

He picked up his padd and rose abruptly. Janeway, startled, met Picard's hazel eyes. He seemed as puzzled as she. Without any further interaction, Admiral Montgomery strode out and was followed by several others. Picard and Paris remained as Janeway gathered her notes.

"Admiral Paris," she said, "permission to speak freely."

He looked troubled, but replied, "Granted."

Janeway put her hands on her hips and stuck her chin out. "That entire briefing lasted less than an hour," she said to them. "We've been gone for seven years. We've accumulated data on over four hundred completely new species. We've had more interaction with the Borg than anyone in this quadrant and we've managed to beat them nearly every time. We've successfully liberated a human woman who was assimilated when she was six years old. We've got an EMH who's exceeded his programming far beyond expected parameters and we've got an entire crew that has performed, not just well, but *exceptionally*. And Starfleet gets all it wants to know in under an hour?"

She was aware that her words were irate, almost belligerent, but she'd been given permission to speak her mind. It was Picard who answered first.

"It's going to be difficult for you to understand this, Kathryn, but . . . while everyone in Starfleet knows about your adventure, and is delighted that you made it safely home despite the incredible odds, you aren't going to be as feted as you might have been had the war not happened."

"It's not that people don't care," put in Paris. "It's that there are so many things we need to be doing to recover. Our resources have been depleted throughout the quadrant. We're helping the Cardassians rebuild, mourning our dead, trying to move on."

"I do understand, Admiral. But the things we've learned can help you do that."

"And they will," said Picard. "Everything we'll need to learn is in your computer databanks. The information will be passed on directly to the experts in their field. The board simply didn't need to keep you here for hours when everyone, including you, has other things to do."

They were trying to soften the blow, of course, and she was going to let them think they had succeeded. "Speaking of which," she said, forcing a smile, "I'd better get back to my ship. Thank you, gentlemen, and good day."

In about a half hour, *Voyager* was going to be crawling with Starfleet personnel whose job it was to learn everything about all the modifications that had been made on the ship in the last seven years, particularly the new technology that Admiral Janeway had given them. As she stood in the turbolift en route to Holodeck One, Janeway wondered why the modifications seemed to take priority over all the other things *Voyager* had brought back with it. The tactical information on the Borg should have been the most vital information, not the shielding technology and other improvements.

The turbolift halted, and she sighed. She was not looking forward to this, but it had to be done. One of the things the Starfleet engineers would analyze would be all the holodeck simulations. Janeway had told her crew that anything they regarded as "personal" could and should be deleted.

The doors to the holodeck hissed open and she entered. Laughter and music reached her ears, and she smiled despite herself.

"Katie, darling!" cried Michael Sullivan, drying his hands with a dish towel. His handsome face was alight with affection. Before she knew it, he'd caught her around the waist, whirled her around twice, and planted a kiss on her mouth. "I've missed you."

"I've missed you too, Michael." Gently, she disengaged herself from his strong arms. "I have some sad news. I won't be able to come to Fair Haven again."

It hurt her, to watch the light fade from his eyes. "Your journey . . . you've made it home then, have you?" At her nod, he said, "Why, Katie, that's wonderful. Just grand. You've been trying for so long. I'm happy for you."

And he was, she had no doubt. But she was sorry for herself. Tenderly, she reached and touched his cheek, feeling the warmth of his holographic skin, the scratch of his holographic beard stubble. He wasn't real, but in a way, he had become very real to her. She had learned to care deeply for him, but where she was going, there was once again a chance for her to learn to care deeply for a living, breathing person.

She stood on tiptoe to kiss him, sweetly, gently, then whispered "Good-bye," turned, and left. She had instructed the computer not to accept any more adjustments to Michael Sullivan from her. It would be up to Tom Paris, the designer of the program, to save or delete the program as he chose.

But as far as she was concerned, when the doors closed behind her, she had left Fair Haven, and all it meant, behind.

And she was surprised at just how painful it was.

The Doctor looked up in surprise as Seven of Nine entered sickbay. She did not appear to be in a good mood. However, with Seven, that was usually a given.

"Implants acting up?" he asked.

"Negative," she replied, then looked a bit discomfited. "I . . . wished to inquire if you needed any assistance."

"My sickbay rush has come and gone," he replied. "Actually, the only thing I'm doing now is writing up my report for Starfleet."

She inclined her blond head. "In that case, I shall leave." Seven turned and strode toward the door.

"Seven, wait a minute," he called after her. She halted. "What about you? I'm certain you will have an extensive report as well, considering your unique position among the crew."

Apparently that was the wrong thing to say. Seven all but glowered. "I completed my report. And I have also been debriefed."

"How was that?" Poor child, he thought. They had probably raked her over the coals, grilled her on everything conceivable.

"It was brief," she replied.

The Doctor considered letting her know that she'd come close to making a pun, then let it pass. "I'm surprised," he said.

"Yes," she said archly. "As am I. Apparently, my 'unique position' warrants no more than forty-five minutes of Starfleet's time." She paused. "Icheb has received notification that he has been accepted into Starfleet Academy."

"Seven, that's wonderful! You must be very proud of him."

"I am."

"But you're going to miss him, aren't you?"

She nodded. "I had not fully taken into account what returning to Earth really means. We will all be . . . scattered. I had not anticipated that Icheb and I would be separated quite so soon."

He wondered where Chakotay fit into all this, but said nothing. "And of course Naomi . . ."

"Naomi Wildman will be returning to her home, to live with both father and mother. It is an appropriate end result."

"But you've been very close to both these children. You're experiencing what some people call 'empty nest syndrome.' You've got nothing to do in astrometrics, and I know what fulfillment you get out of your work. And on top of all of this, you have also never been certain of where you were going to fit in once you return home." He grimaced a little. "Neither am I."

She regarded him thoughtfully. If he had had a heart, it would have raced. Even though he knew that her affections were given elsewhere, the Doctor realized that his infatuation with Seven was not going to go away.

"Would you care for an ice cream sundae?" she asked.

He smiled. "I'd love one."

"I don't want to go home," Naomi Wildman stated flatly. Counselor Deanna Troi was surprised at the vehemence she was sensing from the child.

"I don't blame you," Troi responded, clearly surprising Naomi. "You were born here. *Voyager* is your home."

"You understand," said Naomi, brightening. "I have Mama, Seven, Icheb . . . I don't need a father."

"But you might like to have one," Troi offered.

"Everyone expects me to be so happy about meeting my father, but I'm not. I'm . . . I'm scared. Ktarians are scary-looking."

"Your mother wasn't scared of him. She thought him a wonderful person. Good enough to marry and be the father of her child."

Naomi made a face and looked down at her feet, dangling a few inches off the floor. Deanna waited patiently, but Naomi remained silent.

"You know," Deanna finally said, "we have a lot in common, only backward." Curious, Naomi looked up. "My father was with me until I was seven years old. You aren't going to get to meet your father until you're already seven, but you're luckier than I am. You see, my father died when I was your age. He never got to see me grow up, graduate from the Academy, learn to be a counselor. There was so much in my life that I wished he had been there for, but he wasn't."

Naomi had stopped fidgeting. Her eyes were fixed on Troi's.

"You've got all that time ahead with your daddy. Hasn't he sent you letters about how anxious he is to meet you?"

Naomi nodded.

"He probably thinks he's the luckiest man in the universe. Not only is he getting his wife back, whom he loves very much, but he's getting a beautiful, smart daughter, too."

A shy, soft smile curved Naomi's lips.

"You don't have to love him right away. Love takes time. But don't you think you could try to like him?"

Naomi thought. "I suppose," she said. "I just wish he could have met Uncle Neelix."

"Neelix helped shape the girl you've grown into, Naomi. So in a way, your father *will* get to meet Neelix. And you will never lose your uncle. He will always be part of you."

And at that, the girl rewarded Troi with the biggest smile she'd seen yet from her.

CHAPTER 3

TROI SMILED TIREDLY AS CAPTAIN PICARD HANDED HER A DISH OF ice cream. "I need this after today," she said, spooning up a bite.

"How many people did you speak to?" he asked, then turned to the replicator. "Tea. Earl Grey. Hot."

"About thirty," she said.

He raised an eyebrow. "That's more than you're supposed to see outside of catastrophic situations," he reprimanded, taking his tea and sitting beside her.

"In a way, it is a catastrophic situation," Troi replied. "These people have been without a professional counselor for seven full years, Captain. And they've been through some incredible adventures—some wondrous, some brutally tragic. They've been tremendously isolated and they've adapted by creating their own little world aboard that ship."

"Good or bad?"

She smiled. "Very good. Captain Janeway has almost assumed the rank of a god in some eyes. And after some of the stories I've heard today, that designation seems quite believable."

"Hmm," Picard said.

"And now, with no warning, no time to prepare, to mentally ready themselves for it, they've achieved their goal. They made it back to the Alpha Quadrant. They're going to be with their families in a few days." She paused. "Thank you, by the way, for recommending to the admirals that we not travel home at top speed. *Voyager*'s crew desperately needs the extra time to readjust."

He nodded. "As I suspected. Do you think there will be trouble? Any former Maquis returning with fire in the belly? There was probably a lot of desire for revenge when they heard about the decimation of Tevlik's moonbase."

She shook her dark head and took another bit of ice cream. "No. The division of Federation and Maquis has long since faded. But I do think it likely that they might think of themselves as *Voyager* crewmen first, and Starfleet officers and enlisted second."

"That could be a problem." He leaned back, thinking. "Even Janeway, who's a sterling example of what a captain should be, didn't seem to fully grasp how much things had changed—though, frankly, Admiral Montgomery was unnecessarily harsh with her. It's a shame, really. At any other time in recent history *Voyager*'s homecoming would be the most important thing to happen to Starfleet in any given year. Now, their safe return is barely a footnote."

Troi's large, dark eyes were somber as she regarded her captain. "Some of them are beginning to understand that. And it's not helping their readjustment any."

"I can imagine." He made his decision. "Tomorrow, I want you back on *Voyager* for the duration of its trip back to Earth. Those people are going to need you. You have my permission to regard this as a catastrophic-level duty assignment."

"Aye, sir." She answered quickly enough, and he was certain that she was more than willing to help, but he knew these next few days were going to be difficult for her.

"And Deanna," he said, teasing gently, "it's not going to be easy. Better fortify yourself with more chocolate."

Janeway sat in her ready room, pondering. In sixteen hours, they would be in orbit around Earth. She and her senior staff had all been debriefed. Torres's had taken the longest—four hours. Janeway had the dubious honor of coming in second. Everyone else had been dismissed after a half hour or forty-five minutes. Hardly enough for an extended away mission, let alone one that had lasted seven years. . . .

Stop it, she told herself. *What did you expect? Medals? A parade down the streets of San Francisco? Fireworks? These people are coming off a brutal war. Be grateful that you all got home safely. You didn't do this to win praise, you did this to keep a promise—to return your crew to their families.*

Her door chimed. "Come," she called.

Chakotay entered. He was clad in his dress uniform, as was she. "It's time," he said.

Janeway had thought about doing this via intercom, but decided that she wanted to do it in person. So her entire crew was assembled in Cargo Bay Two. They were all clad in dress uniform. Some of them wore medals. She let Chakotay precede her, heard the tinny whistle announcing her entrance.

"Captain on deck!"

The crew snapped to attention. Janeway savored the picture, her eyes roaming from one individual to the next. This was going to be bittersweet. She strode to the front of the room and stood behind the podium.

"At ease," she said. They relaxed. She looked at the padd she held in her hand, then carefully placed it down. Even though she had spent hours crafting the speech, she now realized she didn't want to use it. She would speak from the heart. Her crew deserved it.

"Seven years ago, I made a decision that left this crew and this fine ship stranded thousands of light-years from everything we knew. Even then, I held a firm conviction that this day, today, would come. The day when we are but a few hours away from Earth, and from finally seeing our loved ones. We have faced many challenges, learned many things. We've lost some fine people." Her eyes found Icheb and little Naomi, Gilmore and Lessing from the *Equinox*. She smiled. "And added some new crew members along the way. Each of you has contributed in so many ways to making this incredible journey the astounding feat it was. It has been a true honor to be your captain. I have asked and asked, and asked yet more from you, and you always continued to astonish and amaze me with your resourcefulness, your courage, and your compassion. But now, the journey is done. This unique voyage has, finally, ended. We have come home."

Her throat closed up and she blinked hard. She reached for the padd, found the spot she wanted. "I'd like to close with a quote from the Earth author T. S. Eliot. 'Not fare well, but fare forward, voyagers.' " She looked out into the sea of faces, all known, all loved, and knew that she would miss them and this ship desperately. "May we, voyagers all, fare forward. Godspeed."

The room erupted in applause. She saw that her mixture of pain and joy was reflected on almost all the faces of her crew. Many were weeping openly. Chakotay stepped forward and motioned for quiet.

"Captain," he said, "if you can spare the time, the crew has a request. They would all like the opportunity to make their personal farewells to you now, while they are all still formally crew members of *Voyager*."

Janeway had thought her heart full, but now it overflowed. For the rest of her life, she knew, she would remember this: walking down the seemingly endless line, sharing laughter, hugs, handshakes, slaps on the back. She tried to brand each face into her brain, every word, every expression. Whatever her own new voyage held for her, it would be hard pressed to measure up to the exquisite, painful joy of this single precious moment.

There was to be a "welcome home" dinner for all crew members and up to four guests held at Starfleet Headquarters in San Francisco. Because this was a hugely complicated gathering to arrange at such short notice, all crew were requested not to leave the ship in order to greet family and friends until the dinner.

"This is driving me nuts," Harry Kim confided to Paris, stalking up and down the small room like a caged animal. "Why can't I see them?"

"Starfleet red tape," said Paris, cooing at little Miral. She wasn't buying it. She glared at him, then opened her mouth and wailed lustily. "That's one thing I haven't missed in the last seven years." He rose and thrust Miral into Harry's arms. "Here. I don't want to let all that rhythmic, soothing pacing go to waste."

"You're lucky," said Kim, cradling the baby awkwardly and almost shouting to be heard over her crying. "You got to see your dad before anyone else on this ship."

"Yeah, but it could have gone worse," said Paris. He grinned a little as Miral's angry cries faded into satisfied murmuring. "And don't forget, I'm getting to meet a Klingon mother-in-law tonight."

"And how is that worse for you than it is for me?" challenged B'Elanna, coming out of the bathroom adjusting her dress uniform. "Hey, Starfleet, you're pretty good with her. Too bad you won't be around to baby-sit anymore."

Kim smiled, feeling a rush of affection for both of these people. The terms he and B'Elanna used, which had once marked their differences, had become pet names between two dear friends.

"Don't worry, Maquis," he said. "I hope to visit you guys often."

"Door's always open, Harry." Paris rose and took his daughter from Harry's arms, then turned to B'Elanna. "Showtime," he said.

"Seven, what are you doing here?" said the Doctor, adjusting his dress uniform. "I thought that you and Chakotay would already be at the party."

"Commander Chakotay will be anxious for some time alone with his Maquis friends. I will not be attending," she said stiffly. "I have come to complete the cataloguing I began earlier." As if she were the head of sickbay and not he, Seven slipped easily into the Doctor's chair.

"What about your aunt? Surely she'll be there tonight."

"I received a transmission from her. She is unwell and also will be unable to attend." Seven's fingers were flying over the controls, but now they paused in their frantic motions. "She has extended an invitation for me to visit her once I am . . . settled in."

"Seven," the Doctor said gently, "please tell me you are going to go see her." Seven did not answer. "She's the only family you have!"

"*Voyager* was my family," she blurted before she could retract the statement. A blush colored her cheeks. "And now my family is dispersed. There is no purpose to my attending tonight, and these catalogues—"

"Are what we call busywork and are almost completely super-fluous," the Doctor said firmly. "And there is actually quite a vital purpose to your attending tonight."

Surprised, she looked up at him. "What?"

"Have you never thought that I don't have any family, either?" he said. "Oh, I'm certain I'll soon be hugely sought-after in the medical community, with my vast store of knowledge and experience. But tonight, it's all about friends and family. I won't have anyone to talk to at the banquet."

He extended an arm. "I would be honored if you would grant me the favor of your company this evening, Miss Seven of Nine."

For a long, long moment, he thought she would refuse. He expected her to refuse, actually. But finally, an uncertain smile curved her full lips, and that smile reached her eyes.

"I will require a change of uniform," she said.

Kim materialized in an enormous hall. Flags representing every Federation member planet hung from the high, arched ceiling. Windows opened to the San Francisco sky, and the muted hues of twilight vied with artificial lighting for the right to illuminate this vast chamber. Soft music played in the background, and more tables than Kim had ever seen in one place stretched the length of this great hall. Kim gaped openly for a moment. He had never seen this room before; it was reserved for high ceremony. He supposed that Starfleet had, after the cursory briefings, come to the realization that *Voyager* rated such kudos.

Quickly, though, he forgot about the opulence of the room and began scanning the crowd, looking for those whose faces he had kept in his mind for seven years.

So many people! Out of the corner of his eye, he saw big, jolly Chell squeal happily as he rushed to embrace two blue Bolians. Little Naomi, standing close beside a beaming Samatha Wildman, formally stuck her hand out to a towering Ktarian male who gently accepted it. Vorik stood politely conversing with three Vulcans. They appeared to be strangers, but, knowing Vulcans, Kim was willing to bet they were his family.

Captain Janeway was hugging two women at the same time. One was an older woman who looked a lot like her, and the other was a little younger than she. They had to be her mother and sister.

Over there was Chakotay, his expression a mixture of joy and sorrow, as he embraced men and women who Kim assumed were fellow Maquis members. And there was the Paris family. Kim didn't recognize the older, attractive woman, but guessed she was Tom's mother. Standing next to them was a tall, handsome man with black hair and a dark complexion.

Harry stared. Was this B'Elanna's father, after all these years? B'Elanna looked as if she were trying to decide whether to punch the man or throw herself in his arms.

He never saw which she did because at that moment, a beloved voice cried, "Harry! Oh, Harry!"

Harry whirled and saw an elderly Asian couple threading their way through the crowd. When their eyes met, the woman lifted a long, rectangular box over her head. He knew what it was, and tears sprang to his eyes. She had brought his clarinet.

"Mom! Dad!" he cried, and rushed to embrace them fiercely. And even as he hugged them, he saw another person he had never forgotten, despite the intervening years, the resignation at never seeing her again, and the things he had shared with other women who had entered his life. He saw a lovely face framed by curly dark hair, and large eyes filled with tears even as her mouth curved wide in a smile of joy.

Libby.

Voyager's crew had all finally come home.

CHAPTER 4

TUVOK MATERIALIZED IN THE FRONT HALL OF HIS OWN HOME. THE colors were slightly different. He took a moment to note the changes his wife had made in his absence. Instead of the muted, dark purple, there were now shades of blue and green. The ancient urn that had stood in the hallway alcove had been moved to the top of the stairs. It had been replaced by a landscape painting of the Voroth Sea. Looking closer, he saw that it bore the name of his youngest child. He raised an eyebrow. T'Pel had always had an eye for fine art, and it was good to see that the child had not squandered her talents.

"They told us that you did not wish us to travel to Earth to greet you, once Sek had completed the *fal-tor-voh*," a soft, female voice said.

Despite himself, despite his years of discipline, Tuvok could not suppress a quickening of his pulse. He did not permit himself to turn around immediately.

"That is correct," he said, keeping his voice modulated. "There was no logic in disrupting the present status of your lives for an excessive and unnecessary human-inspired celebration. Once I was cured, I would then be debriefed and able to return to Vulcan shortly thereafter."

"I agree, husband," said T'Pel, stepping into the light as he turned around. "There was no reason to rush this reunion. I have waited seven years for your safe return. A few days more is insignificant. I trust that the *fal-tor-voh* was successful?"

"Entirely. Sek is a worthy son and performed the mind-meld admirably."

He moved toward her. They were only inches apart, now. Her shining brown eyes, tranquil as a pool on temple grounds, met his evenly. Slowly, Tuvok lifted his right hand and extended the first two fingers. T'Pel hesitated, and then lifted her own hand. Their fingers touched.

He did not wish it, but something stirred within him. Tuvok was still recovering from the effects of the recently cured neurological dysfunction. The mind-meld with Sek had been a balm to an injury. Peace had descended upon Tuvok's restless, churning mind once more as his son reached and touched his mind, calmly eradicating all hints of the degeneration.

A faint frown rippled across T'Pel's smooth, lovely face as she sensed the agony and confusion he had undergone . . . and something more. Something that was, no doubt, directly caused by the lingering effects of the condition.

"On the other hand," T'Pel continued smoothly, "it is also illogical to behave as if you had not been gone for so long a time, is it not?"

"Most illogical," he agreed. Her flesh was warm against his, her mind open to him through the intimate touch of finger against finger.

Although he had, most inconveniently, undergone *Pon farr*

very recently aboard *Voyager,* where the primal desires thus roused were slaked by a holographic version of the female now standing before him, Tuvok experienced an echo of that powerful desire. Sensing his thoughts, T'Pel lifted an eyebrow in inquiry.

There was no need for words. As he accompanied his wife to their bedchamber, Tuvok reflected on how, under certain extreme circumstances, the descent of *Pon farr* was not always required to elicit the mating response.

Janeway stood looking around at her austere, clean apartment. She was partly amused, partly despairing. This new place was waiting for her in San Francisco, courtesy of Starfleet Command. All the senior staff had been offered that option. Some had declined, others accepted. For the moment, Janeway had said yes, and was now doing her best to decorate it with the furniture and knickknacks her mother had recovered when she had been given up for lost. They had stayed in the attic in the house in Indiana, and now they looked rumpled and pitiful in the gleaming Starfleet-provided apartment. Janeway sighed.

The door chimed. "Come," she said, surprised—Who knew she was here?—and turned to greet her first visitor.

The door hissed open, and Mark Johnson stood there.

For a moment, she didn't breathe. "Hello, Kathryn," he said gently. "I hope it was all right for me to come. I spoke with your mother and she seemed to think so."

"Mark," she said, recovering. "Yes, of course. It's so good to see you."

He held out his arms and she went to him. Even as she laid her head on his chest, she saw the light wink against the simple gold band on his left finger. She knew he'd gotten married, and oddly, she felt no pain at the thought. Only pleasure that he had found someone, again, to love. He was a good and gentle man, and deserved it.

"I'm so glad you're home," he said, his breath on her hair. They pulled apart, and Janeway saw that his eyes, too, were filled with tears.

"Thank you for coming," she said, stepping away. "Can I make you some coffee?" she asked, and then had a brief moment of distress when she realized that she didn't know where the replicator was in this new place.

"No, thanks. Hang on—I've got something of yours I need to return to you."

While he was gone, Janeway took the opportunity to recover. She hadn't realized how much she had missed him. More correctly, she hadn't *let* herself realize how much she had missed him. But now, seeing him after all this time, feeling him warm and strong against her—

"Stop it, Kathryn," she told herself in a low voice. "No sense wasting energy on could-have-beens." And yet, it was difficult.

A dog's bark shattered her thoughts and she turned. Sitting beside Mark in the front room, a little heavier than she remembered and graying around the muzzle, was Molly.

"Oh, Molly!" she called, kneeling and opening her arms to the animal. Molly looked uncertainly up at Mark, then back at Janeway. The Irish setter tilted her head quizzically.

Janeway forced a smile through the pain. Of course, Molly wouldn't remember her. It had been seven years. She straightened and laughed uncomfortably.

"That was a little foolish, I suppose," she said. "You've been her master for most of her life."

Mark smiled his easy, comfortable smile. "Hey, I've only been dog-sitting. She's always been yours. I can tell you who took the puppies, if you'd like to know. Everyone was so excited about your return. They feel like they own a celebrity dog. They'd be honored if you'd visit."

"Maybe I will," she said, though in truth, she thought she probably wouldn't. She didn't know those dogs, those people. So much had changed. "Keep her, Mark. You've loved her and taken care of her for seven years. She's your dog, now."

He seemed about to argue, then took a long look at her and nodded. That, at least, hadn't changed. He knew her so well. He always had been able to see through her bravado. It was that quality that had made her fall in love with him in the first place.

She sat on the couch that clashed horribly with the surroundings and indicated that he do likewise. Molly, relaxed and calm, began to sniff Janeway's unpacked things.

They sat, stiffly. There were only a few inches of distance between them, but it might as well have been kilometers. Neither spoke for a while.

Finally, Mark broke the uncomfortable silence. "Kathryn, this is awkward. For both of us. You know that if I believed you were alive and coming home, I'd have waited."

"Of course I do," she said swiftly. "You did nothing wrong, Mark. I'd have done the same thing."

He looked haunted. "Would you? I wonder. It's just— Kathryn, we were friends long before we were anything else. I have always admired and respected you, and that hasn't changed. If anything, it's grown. You're . . . amazing to me. I think about you every day. Carla understands how important a person you were in my life. I'd like for you to continue to be in my life as it is now, with Carla and Kevin."

"Kevin?"

"Our son." He laughed. "He's a petty tyrant, but we love him.

I'd like for him to get to know his aunt Kathryn." His eyes were somber. "Will he?"

There was no question in her mind, only happiness. She extended her left hand. He took it, squeezed it. "Of course," she said. "I wouldn't miss being a part of that for the universe, Mark."

And for the first time since he'd walked back into her life, the ghost and shadows around his eyes lifted, and he smiled from his heart.

She had dinner with the Johnsons that night, and after a few strained minutes, Janeway found herself feeling right at home. The toddler Kevin was indeed a petty tyrant, but all was forgiven when he smiled. Not even Naomi Wildman had been so cute at that tender age.

Mark's wife Carla was a lovely woman. She was a little younger than Janeway or Mark, with a sharp brain, a cheerful grin, and an easy manner that Janeway responded to immediately. Molly was obviously well loved and looked after, and as the evening progressed she seemed to remember Janeway a little bit more. It felt good.

A brief crisis came when Carla, who had tried to actually bake a soufflé, yelped in the kitchen. She stuck her head out. "Mark, Kathryn . . . I'm so sorry. The dessert is a total disaster. I should have replicated it. I'm sorry," she repeated.

"Carla, it's all right. I'm so full from your delicious dinner that I probably wouldn't have done it justice anyway," Janeway said. It was no lie; her stomach was straining.

Carla seemed unduly distressed by the fallen soufflé. Janeway sensed it was more than just a failed dessert. Mark suggested that they take coffee outside. It was a balmy summer evening, and the Johnsons lived in the country. Janeway eased back in her chair and inhaled the redolent scents of roses and grass. Mark had gone in to get them each a second cup of coffee, and Carla took the opportunity to be blunt.

"I was quite jealous, you know," she said, cutting to the chase.

Janeway looked over at the younger woman. "Really?"

She nodded her head earnestly. "Really. It was always Kathryn this, Kathryn that. He had such a great relationship with you that it was like you were always present, even when it was just the two of us."

Janeway put her elbows on the table and regarded the young woman intently. "I'm no threat to you, Carla."

"Oh!" Carla's eyes flew wide. "Oh, Kathryn, no, that's not what I meant! I meant that you seemed like such a wonderful person that I was jealous of Mark for having been so close to you. I wished I'd known you, too. I wished I'd had a Kathryn Janeway to go to with all my problems. And now—well, look at you! You're a hero, and my house is a mess and my soufflé fell!"

No wonder Mark had fallen in love with this beautiful woman. What a generous spirit she had. On impulse, Janeway rose and embraced her. Carla enthusiastically returned the hug.

Mark returned with two steaming mugs of coffee and grinned at the sight.

"You're a lucky man, Mark Johnson," said Janeway, pulling apart a little way from Carla. The younger woman's eyes shone with pleasure.

"Yes," he said, looking from one of them to the other. "Yes, I certainly am."

She hadn't wanted to leave, and it was clear that Mark and Carla didn't want her to, either. They even offered her the guest bedroom as the night grew late and threw in a tempting offer of homemade waffles for breakfast, but she declined. When she transported out, to rematerialize in the strange, unfamiliar room, Janeway wished she had accepted their generous invitation. She had been back on Earth for weeks now, and yet tonight, with Mark and her new, wonderful friend Carla, was the first time she felt really "at home."

As she puttered about, delaying getting into the strange bed, she realized what it was that made her so reluctant to claim this space as her own. She missed *Voyager*. She missed the sounds of the vessel, the feel of the chairs and the bed, the wide starfield that she would often gaze at for a long time before finally drifting off into a restless sleep.

It was late, almost two in the morning. Yet, she sat down and tapped the small viewscreen on the table. The sound would be soft, she knew. If he didn't want to answer, he wouldn't have to. No insistent combadges, not anymore.

His face appeared on the screen. Like her, he was fully dressed and seemed wide awake. "Hi," he said, smiling.

"Hi," she said feeling her own lips stretch into a grin.

"Couldn't sleep?" asked Chakotay.

"Nope."

"Funny, me neither."

"Too quiet. No Borg attacks at all."

"Know what you mean. And no starfields to go to sleep by."

She shook her head.

"Want to come over for some coffee?" he asked.

"The real stuff?"

"But of course. That's half the reason we came home, isn't it?" His smile faded slightly.

"What is it?" Janeway asked. Over the last seven years, she

had learned to recognize every expression that flitted over that dark, handsome face.

"I'm planning on taking a trip shortly," he said. "A very important one. I was wondering if you'd like to accompany me."

The ship that Chakotay jokingly called the "Alpha Flyer" zipped along with a smoothness that belied its rough exterior. Janeway relaxed and leaned back in the copilot's seat of the little craft.

"Nice ship, Captain Chakotay," she said. He threw her a quick grin.

"Always told you I wanted a nice little ship of my own," he said. "You know, as a first officer, you're not half bad."

"Coming from the best first officer it's been my pleasure to know, I'm flattered." The stars streaked by as they sat in comfortable silence for a while. Finally, Janeway said, "I understand that all the former Maquis on *Voyager* were offered the opportunity to return to Starfleet, with all rank returned."

"It was a generous officer," said Chakotay, reaching down and tapping the console.

"Will it be one you accept?"

"I don't know yet." He turned to look at her, and his dark eyes were serious. "I hadn't expected our return to be without its difficulties, but I confess, I'm surprised at some of the emotions it's stirring up."

"I know exactly what you mean," said Janeway, thinking of Mark, Carla, and little Kevin. "I don't think we realized just how sheltered we were on *Voyager*."

"I had a chance to meet with Sveta and some of the other Maquis at the banquet. For them, it's all the past, but for me—

well, not having been there, not having gone through it with them, it's still pretty raw."

Even at their most intimate over the last seven years, Chakotay had never spoken quite so freely. Janeway was touched by his confidence. She had thought they had grown close, and was certain that they had, but clearly, that barrier between captain and crewman had blocked off more than she had thought.

She took a look at the coordinates of their destination. Somehow, it seemed familiar. Then Janeway realized where they were headed, and her stomach tightened. Chakotay was bringing her along with him to face some of the demons of his past.

They did not speak the rest of the time, but sat, each lost in private thoughts. Finally, Chakotay dropped out of warp and into orbit around a small moon. He leaned back, took a deep breath, and exhaled slowly through his mouth. Janeway recognized it for what it was; a calming breath, to steady himself for what lay ahead.

He straightened, resumed control, and took the Alpha Flyer down. Tom Paris couldn't have made a smoother landing, and when he set them down gently, Janeway looked out at the deceptive beauty of this moon that housed such a horror.

They got out and walked toward a tall standing stone. On it was a bronze plaque. "I didn't know Starfleet had marked this yet," Janeway said, her voice hushed and reverent as if she was in a holy place. In a very real sense, she was.

"They haven't," Chakotay replied, his own voice soft. "Sveta and some of the other Maquis did this all on their own."

Strangely, Janeway felt stung by the comment. "I'm certain Starfleet would have gotten around to making this official," she said.

"I'm not. There's a lot on their minds right now. Memorializing people once considered traitors can't be very high on their list."

The plaque read:

On this site, on Stardate 50953.4, one of the most brutal massacres of the Dominion War took place. For many months, Tevlik's moon had been a secret base for the group calling themselves the Maquis, who fought a private war based on their highest morals and ethics against the Cardassians, whom they regarded as the enemy. It was considered a safe place, and many brought their families here to protect them from repercussions. Due to the betrayal of one of their leaders, a Bajoran called Arak Katal, the entire population of the base was wiped out by a surprise Cardassian attack.

Four thousand, two hundred and fifty-six men, women, and children were slaughtered. The Cardassians took no prisoners.

This plaque is to commemorate the dead. May they never be forgotten, and may the principles for which they stood always be remembered.

There followed a list of names, many that Janeway recognized. She'd been told about the attack, of course, but she hadn't realized there had been whole Maquis families based here. Nor had she fully appreciated the sheer number of lives lost. And she had not known that they were betrayed by one of their own. For a moment, she and Chakotay stood in reverent silence.

Finally Janeway said softly, "What became of Arak?"

"No one knows," answered Chakotay. "He could have been a Cardassian agent, like Seska. Or he could have had other reasons for betraying us. According to Sveta, he simply disappeared. He had better never show his face in this quadrant," he added, his voice suddenly harsh and angry. "I know many who'd kill him on sight. I'd be one of them."

"With B'Elanna right behind you," said Janeway. "I hope it doesn't come to that. I'd hate to have to visit you in prison for the rest of your life."

He looked at her and smiled, a little. There was no hint that there had been a base here. All equipment had been salvaged long ago; all the dead, identified and buried. All that remained was this standing stone and the plaque.

"Will we ever move beyond this?" Janeway suddenly said, the words bursting from her. "We claim to be so advanced, to value peace and good relationships with all species. And yet, I stand here, and I see this, and I wonder."

"I wonder too," said Chakotay. "Peace is precious. But there is such a thing as too high a price for peace."

She reached out and slipped a comforting arm around his waist. His arm came up and draped across her shoulders. They stood like that, side by side, wordlessly thinking about peace, and prices, and other destinies.

"If I hadn't been hiding in the Badlands," said Chakotay, "I'd have been operating from this base. It's more than likely that my name would be there, too."

Janeway shuddered at the thought. "Do you feel guilty that you didn't die with them?" she asked, softly.

He didn't answer at once. Finally, he said, "No. I was where destiny placed me. I shirked nothing. But I desperately wish that Starfleet had seen what we had seen earlier, that the Cardassians were not to be trusted. Then maybe all these good people would still be alive."

Slowly, they turned and walked back to the small ship. As

they lifted off, Janeway turned to Chakotay and said, "I'm glad our destinies coincided, Chakotay. It was a privilege to have you at my side these past seven years."

He smiled. "And it was a privilege to serve with you, Captain."

She laughed and held up a hand in protest. "Kathryn. I'm not your captain anymore."

"Ah," he joked, "you'll always be Captain to me."

Suddenly serious, she looked into his dark eyes. "I hope not," she said.

On Earth, in the state of Colorado, little Kevin Johnson whimpered in his sleep. Above him, a small mobile turned, emitting soft nursery music. Inside his crib, the toddler tossed and turned. Beneath tightly shut lids, his eyes darted back and forth. His cheeks flushed, then paled, then flushed again. But he did not awaken.

Inside his body, racing along his veins, something alien went about its programmed duty. Microscopically tiny, perfectly constructed machines came to life, replicated, latched on to blood cells. With each second, more and more of them appeared and began systematically replacing human anatomy with machine.

And on his soft, fragile baby's cheek, a spidery Borg implant erupted.

To Be Continued